HIS FORBIDDEN ROYAL HEIR

CAROL MARINELLI

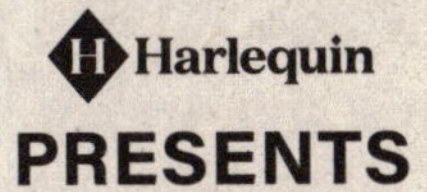

PRESENTS

Recycling programs for this product may not exist in your area.

ISBN-13: 978-1-335-61404-9

His Forbidden Royal Heir

For questions and comments about the quality of this book, please contact us at CustomerService@Harlequin.com.

Harlequin Enterprises ULC
22 Adelaide St. West, 41st Floor
Toronto, Ontario M5H 4E3, Canada
www.Harlequin.com

HarperCollins Publishers
Macken House, 39/40 Mayor Street Upper,
Dublin 1, D01 C9W8, Ireland
www.HarperCollins.com

Printed in Lithuania

1 2 3 4 5 6 7 8 9 10 LIT 28 27 26 25

“Tell me who you are, Rafiq, before I get in the car.”

“Very well.” He nodded. “I am royal. I know it can sound a little daunting…”

“How royal?” She cut him off with a question, thought back to the deference with which he’d been treated, as if nothing had been too much trouble from the second he’d arrived. And now this security detail, the car, the everything. “How royal are we talking, Rafiq?”

“I am…” Oh, she looked up at him and somehow knew he was more than a minor royal, more than some vague prince, and then he confirmed it. “I am the crown prince of Al-Zahir.”

“Crown prince…” Liliana frowned. “Does that mean…?” Her throat felt too tight, and there was this need almost to put her hand down low on her stomach, but she fought it. Did not want to give him a hint of the chance life that for the past few weeks she’d been trying to deny. But if Rafiq was a crown prince, did that mean…? “You’re the heir?” she checked.

“Correct.”

And it was too much.

Just by far too much.

God alone knew what it meant if she was pregnant.

Carol Marinelli recently filled in a form asking for her job title. Thrilled to be able to put down her answer, she put "writer." Then it asked what Carol did for relaxation and she put down the truth—"writing." The third question asked for her hobbies. Well, not wanting to look obsessed, she crossed her fingers and answered "swimming"—but, given that the chlorine in the pool does terrible things to her highlights, I'm sure you can guess the real answer!

Books by Carol Marinelli

Harlequin Presents

Scandalous Sicilian Cinderellas

The Sicilian's Defiant Maid
Innocent Until His Forbidden Touch

Heirs to the Romero Empire

His Innocent for One Spanish Night
Midnight Surrender to the Spaniard
Virgin's Stolen Nights with the Boss

Wed into a Billionaire's World

Bride Under Contract
She Will Be Queen

Rival Italian Brothers

Italian's Pregnant Mistress
Italian's Cinderella Temptation

Visit the Author Profile page at Harlequin.com for more titles.

HIS FORBIDDEN ROYAL HEIR

PROLOGUE

Sheikh Prince Rafiq of Al-Zahir had been born third in line to the throne and was happy to be so. He didn't mind that his parents' attention fell mainly on his older brother.

'Khalid was born to be king,' his father had explained.

On the long summer school holidays, home from England, where they were schooled, Khalid readily headed off for lessons on Al-Zahir's history, or to study the strict edicts he would one day uphold. Rafiq, though he was tutored extensively too—just in case—was afforded more freedom. A lot of his summers had been spent in the desert, being taught by the elders or riding his horses, but lately his desert time was interspersed with athletic meets.

Rafiq loved to run, more specifically he loved sprinting. Long limbed, a naturally athletic build, he had the explosive power required for rapid speed. Aged eleven he was causing a stir with his track times.

Khalid was serious like their father, a bit of a geek, the good son; however you wanted to put it, Khalid studied and followed the rules meticulously.

Rafiq, on the other hand, painted outside the lines. He was very bright but challenged everything. Even so, there was a certain allure to Rafiq. He got by on charm and could eke out a smile from anyone.

Even their serious, rather grim father.

Still, horses and athletic meets weren't the only thing on Rafiq's mind that summer when the brothers arrived back at the palace.

'Finally,' Rafiq said to his older brother. 'I get to find out the sex edicts.'

'You are going to be so disappointed.' Khalid laughed.

As it turned out, Khalid was right.

The edicts were many and long, more a list of dos and don'ts and intricate rules that took a full week to get through when he would far rather be in the desert.

'I am never marrying…' A sulking Rafiq knocked on Khalid's study door and went in.

'Told you.' Khalid smiled but did not look up from his studies.

'I mean it,' Rafiq said and lay on a sofa with his hands behind his head, going over in his mind what he'd been taught today. 'What's the point in marrying if you can also keep a harem?'

'It's just the way things are done.' Khalid shrugged.

'Do you think our father keeps one?'

'I have no idea.'

'Do you think he has a mistress?'

Khalid looked up from the computer. 'You had the lesson on discretion today, yes?'

Rafiq nodded.

'Then you would have been taught that, if he does have a mistress, it is not for us to know.'

'Or our mother.' Rafiq scowled, not liking what he'd been taught.

'The discretion rules are to protect her.'

'Well, I'm not having my bride chosen for me, or getting married before I'm twenty-one. I want to be breaking records and pulling in medals.'

'You can still run, but of course you will have to marry young,' Khalid told him. 'You're second in line to the throne now.'

Khalid had swallowed; their grandfather had recently died, and their father was now king.

Second in line felt a little too close for comfort.

'If I die it will fall to you,' Khalid reminded him.

'Don't talk like that.' Rafiq frowned.

'But it's true, and with all the trouble with Al-Nawar the lineage needs to be secured. Of course you will marry.'

Al-Nawar was the neighbouring country. Usually a peaceful land, their despot king had been causing problems and there were urgent talks underway. Their father was even more serious and grim.

Life felt a little less carefree of late.

Rafiq, his hands still behind his head, had a sudden feeling of dread and looked over to his brother, who was still working away on his computer.

Nothing would happen to him, Rafiq told himself. After all, Khalid was born to be king.

More than that though, Rafiq loved his brother so.

CHAPTER ONE

CROWN PRINCE RAFIQ thanked the chauffer then climbed the steps of his Belgravia residence, craving solitude.

He could see one of his security officers parked in the street, and even if it was his own people watching he remained solemn and dignified.

Rafiq never let his guard down, even amongst his own.

This visit to London had been filled to the brim with high-stakes meetings—navigating the political whirl, as well as ceremonial duties. And it had not been his usual success, not that he let it show. His features remained impassive until the large black door to his London home was safely closed.

'*La'nat*,' he sighed, leaning on the door.

Damn.

Tomorrow Rafiq would return to Al-Zahir empty-handed. He had arrived on the cusp of securing a landmark cultural exchange to showcase the island's rare pearls and had intended to have it locked in. But as always, Al-Nawar, the neighbouring land, was proving to be the thorn in delicate negotiations.

All his life Al-Nawar had been the thorn.

Rafiq knew his dark mood had little to do with the poor progress on the cultural exchange though.

It felt as if his life was a succession of anniversaries.

Some were well-known and public facing, like the national day of mourning for Khalid, which would take place just over three months from now.

Others were more private and went unacknowledged.

A few days ago, it had been the anniversary of Khalid's capture.

Today it was Rafiq's.

The anniversaries did not end there.

Nine months from now, the people of Al-Zahir would celebrate the anniversary of Rafiq's miraculous escape…

Rafiq, now surrounded by security and next in line to the throne, felt far from free.

Something alerted him and Rafiq's grey eyes snapped open. The air was not still as the elder tribal warrior would describe…there was no noise, no scent, nothing to denote an intruder, but his senses sharpened and he stared down the elegant hallway.

There was someone here.

He glanced into the receiving room, but his eyes were more drawn to the stairs, and trusting his own instinct, he headed up to the private areas of the luxurious home.

Expecting an errant maid but prepared for anything, he pushed open the study's heavy door and saw a woman standing by the window gazing down at the tree-lined street and the embassy cars below.

Princess Yara of Al-Nawar.

'How did you get in?' he demanded, his voice low, eyes narrowing at the intrusion, irritation simmering beneath his warrior-trained calm.

She turned, her gold orchid broach catching the light from the chandelier.

'My security liaised with yours.'

Rafiq hissed in irritation that his security chief had not run this by him. 'I am going to speak with Salar…'

'And make him wonder why you don't want to see me?' Yara warned. 'They think they are doing us a favour by sneaking me in.'

'If word gets out that you are visiting me here our families will have us married within days…'

And that was something neither wanted.

'True,' Yara sighed. 'Still, I had no choice but to take this chance. You do know that the kings are meeting today?'

'Of course.' Rafiq nodded, shrugging his coat off and throwing it onto a pale lemon sofa. 'Hopefully *your* father is in a listening mood. For this exchange to go ahead Al-Nawar needs to—'

'I did not come all this way to discuss the cultural exchange,' Yara sharply interrupted. 'I risked a meeting because there is something you need to know—I believe my father is going to raise the question of us marrying.'

'It is not his place to do so,' Rafiq said, picking up a crystal decanter and pouring a drink. He held up a glass for Yara, who shook her head, but the motion exposed his scarred wrist, and he saw Yara's glance and how she hurriedly looked away—unnecessarily guilty for all he had endured. 'I am the one who calls for marriage—not your father.'

'The thing is…' She swallowed nervously. 'My father…' she explained, her voice quavering. 'Oh, I really should not be telling you this…' She shook her head, baulking at the final hurdle and made to go. 'You're right, I should not have risked things by coming here. I'll leave now…'

'Yara?' Rafiq asked. 'Given what I know, surely you can trust me?'

Closing her eyes briefly, Yara nodded. 'Of course.'

'So, what is it you came here to say?'

'That my father is dying.' Her breath shuddered before she continued, 'He has a year, maybe two.'

Now Rafiq understood why she was here. 'He wants to see us married?'

'Yes.'

La'nat, la'nat—double damn. His day really wasn't going well!

He didn't cuss out loud though, no-one ever glimpsed his true thoughts. 'Fine.' He nodded. 'I shall let my father know that I am calling for you to be…'

'Rafiq, no.' Her dark eyes brimmed with tears. 'I know I said it was what I wanted, but that was a long time ago. I can't go through with it. The thought of…'

'Hey…' Seeing her distress, he lost his stern tone and was kinder, back to the young man he'd been on the day Yara had told him her truth—that her heart did not turn to men. 'We'll never sleep together, Yara. We've been through all this…'

Admittedly they had been lesser royals when they'd made the pact. The stakes not so high. Now two countries were eagerly awaiting this union.

And growing impatient.

Rafiq had been in his final year at university, since his degree had taken longer as he was often competing, when Yara, aged eighteen and in her first year of study, had asked if they could speak.

She had looked upset and nervous and Rafiq assumed she wanted to discuss her uncle, the despot king.

Instead, she had told him her truth and how scared she was.

Rafiq had come up with an answer to her problem and together they had made a pact: when his father pushed for marriage, Rafiq would call for her to be his bride. At the age of twenty-one he'd accepted that sooner rather than later he must marry. Marriage wasn't about love, not when you were royal, and the edicts were clear. And as he'd told Yara—they could both take discreet lovers.

As for heirs?

'Fertility issues.' Rafiq had smiled.

He had smiled far more readily back then.

'Not yet though,' he'd said. 'I want to focus on my running. You have your…' He'd frowned. 'What is it you are studying?'

'Botany.'

'Concentrate on your studies and career. We'll put it off for as long as we can.'

Neither had a clue as to the troubles and dark times ahead.

Yara's father would overthrow his brother and become the king. Al-Zahir had supported the uprising but had paid dearly. Khalid had been kidnapped and later killed, and for a while it had seemed that Rafiq would share his brother's fate.

Nine months after his capture, somehow Rafiq had escaped.

With Yara's father now King of Al-Nawar, the relationships between the two islands had improved. The two kings agreed—Rafiq and Yara's marriage would serve as a means to further unite the countries and better place the troubled history behind them…

However, Rafiq, now thirty-five, still had not called for marriage and as the years had dragged on, relations between the two countries were becoming a little strained.

'I don't think I can go through with it, Rafiq. I just can't do it to Jasmine.'

Rafiq knew she was in a serious relationship with her handmaiden.

'I know that I already live a lie,' Yara continued, 'but to marry you, to go on royal tours, have babies…'

'I get it,' he said. 'I shan't call for marriage.'

Rafiq really was in no rush!

'As if they're going to accept that.'

'They can't force us.'

'Of course they can. We've already kept them waiting long enough and now that my father is dying…'

'What would you have me do here, Yara?' He didn't get what she wanted. 'You don't want to marry me, fine. You do want to marry me, that is fine too.'

'There is another way.' Yara gulped. 'I have been giving it a lot of thought.' Her black eyes met his. 'What if there was a scandal?'

Rafiq frowned as Yara continued.

'A scandal so big that all talk of marriage is delayed…'

Yara really had given this a lot of thought; she just hadn't factored Rafiq or, more importantly, the Al-Zahir people, into her equations. He gave a shake of his head as he declined her suggestion. 'Those days are long since over.' It wasn't just his race times that had caused a stir at meets. Rafiq had earned himself quite a reputation, but that had all been before… 'My people deserve better.'

'Rafiq, please…' she begged, then grew angry. 'Oh, how you've changed. You're so cold now.'

Well, yes, he was tempted to say—the nine months of hell, afforded by her uncle, had rather put paid to his sunny side.

'I can't believe I confided in you.'

'It's good that you did. It's better I know that your father is ill.'

'Not about that.' She stared at him. 'You were prepared to marry just to help me, but now…'

'Now I am crown prince,' he snapped out. 'Now my responsibility is first to my people, and they don't need to see me embroiled in scandal.' He shook his head. 'It's not going to happen.' There was no way he would consider going back to those times. In truth he *couldn't* go back to those times. Back then there had been some lightness and romance to go with sex. Now it was all more clinical and certainly took place only behind closed doors or veils. Now it was just…sex; he allowed no-one near his heart or mind. He shook his head.

'Rafiq, please…'

'No.' While he understood the delicacy and difficulty of Yara's situation, he would not be swayed. And when Rafiq said no, it was final. 'I shall not call for marriage—you have my word on that. And I shall not bow to pressure. You *know* that.'

'I do.' Yara's breath hitched. She, of all people, did know that, for he had kept her secret safe, even in the worst of times. 'It was a year ago today that you were kidnapped, wasn't it?'

Rafiq didn't respond. He could not go there, or discuss it with another.

'I hate what my uncle did to you.'

'He's long gone. Your country has your father now.' His eyes shuttered as the news she had imparted properly hit. 'I am sorry to hear he is ill.'

'Thank you.' She took a shaky breath.

'We just have to hold on.'

She nodded, but there was still doubt in her eyes.

'Yara, for now at least, nothing's changed. I'm not going to call for marriage, no matter what my father says.'

'Okay.'

'So go home, and stop arranging these damn meetings, or we'll be found out and your nightmare could come true.'

She actually laughed and, somewhat appeased, made her way down the stairs and left via the mews. Rafiq moved to the rear of his home and watched the convoy move away, slithering like a black snake through the back street.

He watched as Salar checked the gates were secured then spoke with an officer on the perimeter. Perhaps aware he was being watched, Salar suddenly looked up to the residence and caught Rafiq's eye.

Rafiq did consider telling him not to allow the princess access without first discussing it with him, but he didn't want Salar to get a glimpse that he was anything less than pleased to secretly meet with Yara.

Rafiq trusted no-one.

And with good reason.

So instead of summoning Salar, Rafiq nodded to say all was well.

All was not well on the inside though. Memories, no matter how he tried to resist them, were raining in. Scenes that were surely best forgotten were flashing through his mind. He recalled a worried-looking Salar, here in this very drawing room, informing him that Khalid was missing in the desert and his horse had returned to the tent without its rider. At first it was assumed he'd been thrown from his horse and there were searches underway to locate him.

Unease had gnawed, as it was doing so now, and Rafiq wanted to open the window, just to inhale the frigid air. Instead, he picked up his coat from the couch and pulled it on, deciding to head out for a walk and clear the thoughts swirling in his head.

But the guard in the car would alert Salar, and even if they were discreet he would not be alone.

He still craved solitude. To disappear for a while and get away. And he knew how.

Heading out from the drawing room, he took the stairs down, and then another staircase down to the cellar. He hadn't been here in a very long time.

Fourteen years to the very day.

Khalid had been the one who'd first shown him the tunnel—back then it had been behind a concealed door in the wine cellar. It wasn't in the house plans; even security didn't know it existed.

Their father had told Khalid about it.

His father before him.

The tunnel led to an alley in Knightsbridge near the

underground, Khalid had explained. There was to be no bringing friends home, no sharing this route. It was the only chance a young prince had for a taste of freedom.

Now there was serious protection, the entrance and exits were more like bank vaults and opened by code. Rafiq, though he had never used it, of course knew the correct sequence, but hesitated before entering it.

He'd spent years trying to forget all that had happened.

Entering the code, he heard the grind of metal as the door slid to the side and he stared into the tunnel for the first time since his capture. He relived the shock of finding intruders in his home and being dragged down to the cellar then along the tunnel's dank length.

He stepped in and as the door clanked closed behind him the paltry lighting flickered on. The air held a dank, musty scent: a mix of wet stone, moss and urban dust. The lights flickered, and he felt the vibrations from trains, tubes and city life above. The air was cold and clammy down here, unlike the underground passages in Al-Nawar, where the air had been stifling and every acrid breath had burnt.

Rafiq could not help but compare.

He ran the back of his hand along a damp stone wall and flinched, recalling the chains that had bitten into his ankles and wrists. Remembered for a moment the agony of the sandstone walls against his beaten and whipped flesh.

He came to the exit—more secure than it had been then—and entered the code and stepped into the alley where he'd been bundled into a car and taken to a plane….It was raining, and he looked up to the sky he'd once thought he might never see again and for a moment relished the cold rain falling on his face.

Rafiq walked to the underground and there boarded a semi-empty tube, taking a seat for he rather tended to stand out. So much so that he could already feel someone watching him, and glancing over, caught a man wearing a grey cap looking at him. Rafiq, even dressed in a dark suit and coat and trying to blend in, might as well be wearing desert robes, or in royal regalia…

At the next stop the tube filled, and it was standing room only by the next.

There was something about this man though that had Rafiq's eyes narrow, disliking how he did not step back to let a woman who was boarding past.

She had coppery blonde hair that was damp from the rain and wore a dark trench coat and stilettoes and her lips were pursed in indignation as the man in the cap made it difficult to pass.

'Excuse me, please,' she said rather pointedly, and when the man finally moved, she squeezed past him, coming to a stand near to Rafiq. She went to take hold of the rail above.

It wasn't her beauty that had Rafiq stand.

Simply that she was a lady…

CHAPTER TWO

Liliana Hamilton was not having the best of days.

Her dreadful manager had appeared over her computer screen and given her his lecherous smile. 'I hear you'll be wearing pink for the ball.'

Liliana's back had immediately stiffened but eternally polite, she had smiled. 'That's right.' Her reply was as short as she could make it without sounding rude.

'It's a beautiful gown, though try as I might, I can't quite imagine you in pink.'

She glanced towards her friend and colleague, Margo, who gave her a wide-eyed look that told Liliana she understood her discomfort.

Simon was becoming an issue. A real one. She'd already pulled out of a couple of Christmas dos, pretending she had other plans.

Liliana *should* be living the dream.

She had been employed as a junior designer at a very high-end fashion house in beautiful modern offices in London—there were screens everywhere depicting endless catwalks, the news and gossip around the world. But, instead of putting her talent and education to work with the designers, her time was mainly spent on the phone and computer, answering email enquiries. Occasionally she would go out when they were doing a fashion shoot—but again, she was more the runner than anything to do with the designs. While she knew everyone had to start somewhere, Liliana had known that four years ago when she'd accepted the job!

There were perks—she was party to some incredible discounts and was *expected* to wear her Sunday best each and every day. The heating was hospital grade, and despite the dreary day outside, Liliana wore a flowery dress and high-heeled shoes, with her long strawberry blonde hair worn down. There were some high-end functions too—a ball in spring where the staff got a chance to purchase the label at a huge discount.

But that perk had caused today's discomfort: Simon, her manager, *imagining* her in the dress she would wear.

'Creep,' Margo mouthed as Simon moved off to take a phone call. 'You are bringing…' Margo motioned with her hand, clearly waiting for Liliana to finally spill her mystery man's name. She didn't. 'Your boyfriend…' Margo prompted.

'Of course I am.' Liliana nodded, and knew she had to give herself a little out, just in case. 'If he's still my boyfriend by then.'

'Well, if you two break up then you'd better have found another, or you'll be chasing Simon off all night.'

'Noted.'

Oh, indeed it had been noted and was the very reason Liliana had lied and said she was seeing someone; it had got her out of a lot of uncomfortable invitations for coffee or a drink after work.

She gazed out of the window on a dreary December afternoon and knew soon the skies would be blue, the dress would be pink…and if she was going to stave off Simon, she somehow had to produce a date.

Her friends, and even Simon, had asked for more information about him but Liliana would offer her standard response: 'I don't like discussing my personal life.'

That part wasn't a lie.

Liliana had never liked discussing her *real* personal life—even as a little girl she'd made stories up to explain her father's long stretches of absence and occasional appearances. Of course, her friends at an all-girls school had all too soon found out she'd been lying and then mercilessly teased her. And later, when the real truth had come out, she and her mother had been shunned…

Yes, lying was wrong, but then again, she'd been born of a lie. Her father had had another life—one with a real family, a wife and two children. Liliana was the product of a prolonged affair, and not at all proud of that fact.

In most things she was a sunny, happy person but still struggled to open up and make close friends let alone date. And so at twenty-six years of age she'd never been in a serious relationship. Margo would fall off her seat if she knew that the slightly kooky, high-fashion woman sitting opposite her was a virgin, Liliana was sure.

So she'd decided to do something about it, not just because of Simon. She wanted to grow in herself, and she'd started internet dating but was really having the most terrible time. She took a sneak peek of her phone and saw that the gym guy who seemed a bit gym obsessed, had suggested they meet… How about now? he suggested. He was finishing up at the gym.

'Okay, everyone,' Simon called as he came off the

phone. 'Lucky for you guys we've got a VIP client coming in who wants the place cleared.'

The peasants were being sent home early.

'Hey, Liliana…' Simon was making his way back over and she knew, just knew he was going to suggest they get a coffee or something, and it was then she made the decision—and said yes to meeting with gym guy.

She needed an escort for the ball, even someone with a sense of humour who would agree to play along. It couldn't be worse than Simon, could it?

Actually, yes. It could!

Before her coffee had even made it to her lips, the gym guy had asked her a question so inappropriate that at first Liliana had thought she'd misheard or misunderstood.

No, indeed she'd heard right!

Picking up the huge bag she carried, Liliana had put down money to cover her beverage and she had walked out of the café, pulling on her trench coat as she made her way to the underground. Clipping down the escalators, she was furious. With work, with the world, with slippery wet streets and sudden showers that drenched, with a packed London underground and being jostled on the platform. Oh, she was angry with many things, and especially she was angry with—

'Please…' A suited man stood, a very tall suited man, and gestured his hand towards the seat he had just vacated. 'Have my seat.'

'I'm perfectly capable of standing!' Liliana snapped and then as the rather handsome, unusually polite gentleman gave her a curious look and retook his seat, she regretted her abrupt and rather rude response.

He was just being thoughtful and perhaps more importantly her stilettos were killing her.

But Liliana was especially furious with men—and right now that included the whole lot of them. Her boss, who kept her chained to the phone rather than designing, the manager who kept pursuing her, the appalling date she had just come from, her father…

While she might have listed him last, in her heart she knew on the list of men who had hurt her, her father should come first.

Liliana and her mother had always come a very poor second—his attention had been elsewhere.

She'd tried so hard to be good, to be nice, to be funny, to be invisible, to be polite…anything that might make him want to stay for Sunday dinner, or take her to the park, or come to the school play.

His constant rejection was the reason she didn't stand up for herself in the real world, or on occasion burst in frustration and succumbed to the social equivalent of road rage, as she'd just done with the handsome man who'd offered her his seat.

Subtly she sneaked a look.

And her breath held in her lungs.

He was stunning.

Thick ebony hair was glossy from the rain and brushed back from a haughty, serious face, and his bone structure was perfection. His high cheekbones and straight Roman nose were perfectly offset by caramel skin and gorgeous silvery grey eyes.

Possibly she sighed.

Yes, utterly stunning, but what the hell was someone in tens of thousands of pounds worth of coat and suit doing on the tube? Oh, she knew that suit was a bespoke one. The stitching along the lapel was divine, and as for his coat—how perfectly it had fallen when he'd stood and offered her his seat.

He could have tried a bit harder, Liliana thought, albeit unreasonably.

Offered his seat twice.

Insisted that she sit down.

And then she let out a little laugh at her own thoughts. The trouble was, she laughed out loud.

Gosh, he must think her both rude and a little mad.

As the tube stopped at the next station the seat next to him freed up. On pointless pride still she refused to sit down, but when the beginning sting of an emerging blister made itself known, she took a seat by his side.

His scent tickled at her nostrils—woodsy, with a citrusy ting and a fragrance she couldn't quite define; she just knew it was a little too exotic for an early Friday evening. Even seated her feet were killing her and she would love to dive in her bag and take out her ballet flats, but her manners were too ingrained for that.

So ingrained that, blushing furiously, she turned her head to apologise. 'I'm sorry about before.'

'Before?'

That frown on his smooth brow was there again; their teeny tiny encounter clearly hadn't been an unforgettable experience for him. 'You offered me a seat.'

'You declined.' He nodded and she was treated to the beauty of a very slight smile. His voice was deep with well-schooled English, yet there was a rich tinge of accent. 'If I remember correctly, you said you were perfectly capable of standing.'

She laughed. 'I'm having a bad day,' she admitted. 'Not that that's any excuse, it's just been a tricky one.'

'Indeed,' he agreed. 'Apology accepted.'

And that was that.

Not quite.

The vision of him remained in her mind, and in that brief exchange she'd glimpsed his perfect full mouth and the dusky shadow on his strong jaw…only it wasn't enough. She ached to turn her head and steal another peek and could feel that she was blushing for no reason. No reason at all, other than that she was overly aware of his thigh aside her own, and when the tube jolted, she braced herself for brief contact from his arm…

It never came.

Despite his proximity, despite his considerable height, not once did they make physical contact, yet somehow merely sitting beside her, he managed to invade every last inch of her personal space.

Nicely so.

When she should still be stinging from that insult of a date, instead she was enthralled and completely aware of this man who sat silently by her side.

He didn't fidget, or tap, or hum as the woman on the other side of her currently was. He didn't read, and from memory he hadn't had headphones in… Liliana stole a glance at his reflection in the black window opposite, just to be sure of that fact. Or was she attempting to meet his gaze…? She had never flirted really, or been so bold, but whatever she was doing didn't work, because he was far too smooth to bother sneaking a peek.

Or simply he gave no thought to the blushing woman seated beside him.

People were starting to get off in droves now as they pulled out of the next station. Apart from one gentleman in a cap standing by the doors it was only them.

Sitting together.

In a deserted tube.

As if they were together.

'Well, this is awkward,' she said and he turned and frowned.

'Excuse me?'

'Us…' She waved to the empty seats and saw that his frown simply deepened. Oh, why did she always say stupid things and talk too much?

'If you would prefer, I can move,' he offered as the train started to pull off. 'I certainly don't want you to feel awkward.'

'Of course not.' She shook her head. 'I was just making a joke. A bad one, clearly, given you didn't get it.'

He offered a brief upturn of his lips—it could not be construed as a smile—and he turned away, the tube grinding from the station, then coming to a halt in a tunnel where they sat for a little while before the driver made an announcement.

'Ladies and gentlemen, this is your driver speaking…'

They were told they were being held due to congestion ahead and would resume moving soon.

Liliana, more than used to it, gave it no thought.

Rafiq could not escape his thoughts.

He wished he'd never keyed in that code, for his mind was still back in the tunnel that had brought him here, or was it back in Al-Nawar and the baking hell of his prison, with the guards taunting him, trying to get him to break?

* * *

'Your king, your father, still refuses to negotiate... He cannot think much of his sons...'

Rafiq already knew his father's stance; before his capture they had argued about it on the phone. If he wouldn't negotiate for Khalid, the heir, there was really little hope for him.

Instead of responding he repeated the question he'd been asking since first captured. 'Where's Khalid?'

For the first time his question was answered.

'Talking,' the guard smirked. 'Khalid sings like a bird.'

Rafiq inhaled sharply, hating the memories that rained on him today. Rather than sit reliving hell, he chose a sweeter option and turned to the woman by his side.

She was very beautiful. Her wavy hair was coiling as it dried, and now that she wasn't blushing in apology, her skin was as pale as porcelain, and he would like to know the colour of her eyes.

'So,' he said. 'You've had a bad day at work?'

She breathed out a silent laugh and turned to him.

Blue.

Her eyes were a very dark blue and framed with long dark lashes, her face so much sweeter than going over memories.

'Every day seems to be a bad day at work at the moment,' Liliana admitted, 'but then it got worse.'

'How so?'

She hesitated, because while she was good at small talk, she didn't open up easily to anyone, and certainly not about things like this. Yet delight flared as he prolonged the conversation. And there was just something about his effect on her that had had her turn her head and smile. ‘I went on a date with this guy I’ve been talking to online.’ She screwed up her nose. ‘I didn’t really want to go but he suggested we meet for coffee and…’ She shook her head. ‘I shan’t bore you with the details.’

Rafiq doubted that she could bore him. Mere moments ago, his mind had been consumed with dark memories. Now, suddenly he was hearing about her world.

And he liked hearing it.

‘I’m Rafiq,’ he said. ‘Can I ask your name?’

‘Lili,’ she said, ‘or Ana.’ He perhaps frowned again because she chose to enlighten him. ‘My actual name is Liliana but it must be a bit of a mouthful because people either call me Lili or Ana. I answer to all three…’

Yes, he liked hearing about her world.

‘So, how come you were meeting this man when you didn’t even want to go?’

‘Because…’ It was a very good question, and she rested her head back against the window behind her and closed her eyes as she accepted what it all boiled down to. ‘I lied.’

‘Oh?’

‘A stupid, pointless lie.’ She sat quietly for a moment pondering the mess she’d landed herself in and then thought of a Sir Walter Scott poem that summed up her situation perfectly. ‘“Oh, what a tangled web we weave, when first we practise to deceive…”’

‘I remember that from school.’

‘I remember it from my mum telling me off!’ Liliana laughed.

‘Do you lie a lot?’

'No,' she said and then thought about it for a moment. 'Maybe. I'm not very…' She paused, because how did she tell him that she wasn't usually so chatty with strangers, and that usually she found so many things awkward and often spoke just to fill gaps? 'When I was little, I used to make up stories.'

'Really?'

'All the time.' She nodded, then paused as the driver informed them they'd soon be moving. 'Very detailed, elaborate ones.' As the tube moved on, so did their conversation, and she couldn't help but wonder how she could speak so easily to this man who she should surely find daunting. Perhaps it was the way he leaned his head in a little as if he really wanted to hear what she had to say as he listened to her tale. 'When I was little, I told all the other girls at school that my father was a captain in the navy and that was why he was away from home so much.'

'He wasn't a captain in the navy?'

'No, he was a vet and married—just not to my mother. He would turn up now and then at a school play and such.'

'Did you tell the girls that he was on shore leave?'

'I didn't get a chance to. I'd already been caught out by then, or rather my father had…' She winced at the memory of her father's wife coming to their door, and the gossip spreading through her village. 'They teased me mercilessly.'

'Children can be cruel.'

'Yes,' she said, then smiled it all away, as if it hadn't mattered a jot. And normally people smiled back when she did that, but Rafiq did not. It was as if he knew her smile was false. 'So, you see,' Liliana quickly concluded, 'I'm not very good at lying.'

The tube could rattle and jolt at times, but as the gaps between stations grew longer there was a nice hum, the occasional peek of the evening sky and the world outside as it moved above ground and then the world disappeared again as the windows turned back to black…and it was really rather relaxing.

Or was it the pleasant, polite man next to her, who simply got her little jokes? At one point she thought the conversation was over.

It was.

Rafiq was not one for idle chatter.

Not anymore.

He'd used to be.

He thought of a whole day spent at the track, watching others, chatting while waiting to be called. Those had been the best of times. Nobody treating him with reverence, and his bodyguard had stayed well back. So much so, Rafiq would forget the other man was there; at meets he was just another athlete.

Liliana didn't know who he was, and it was refreshing.

New.

'So,' he asked, 'what is this tangled web you've weaved?'

Readily she turned back to him. When surely she should be a blushing, bumbling mess, they just spoke so easily, sort of in a new language made just for them, as if they'd known each other for ages rather than just met. There was something patient about his eyes and his smile.

'My manager at work likes me.' She wrinkled her nose.

'Am I right in assuming it's not reciprocated?'

'You're right. But there's a huge fashion ball at the beginning of spring…' She told him the pickle she was in, although he rather frowned at the *pickle* word, but then nodded to let her know that he'd got it.

And then when she told him all about her latest tangled web, she suddenly smiled. 'But the dress is divine.'

Rafiq found that he smiled back, and that was actually a newsworthy event. It wasn't that he never smiled, but they tended to be polite, or official ones, not a slow, soft smile as you looked into the other person's eyes.

For Rafiq there was this rare feeling of freedom as he let his eternal guard down.

'So,' she continued, 'I was talking to this guy online and he seemed nice.'

'Seemed?' His eyes narrowed. 'Did something just happen?'

'No, nothing like that. It was more something he said. I'm not going to tell you what. It's too embarrassing. Suffice to say I got up and walked out…' She paused. 'Well, I paid my half of the bill and got up and walked out.'

'I'm intrigued,' he admitted, 'I want to know what he said to ensure I don't say the same thing!'

'Honestly,' she said and gave a shake of her head, felt his eyes dart to her hair, to her moving curls and then back to her eyes. 'I don't think you ever would.'

For Liliana there was a small revelation occurring. That was it, she realised; that was why she could sit here and easily speak. At a level she hadn't known existed, there was the recognition that this person was safe.

'Anyway, after he said what he did, I dashed for the underground and slid on a puddle. I was just all cross with the world, oh, and men in particular, and then you offered me a seat…'

'As any gentleman would do.'

'Not in my world.'

'Then you're in the wrong world.'

Their eyes met again and it was dizzying for a second—as if her very soul was being examined. And, what's more, she was examining his. Even to herself she could not articulate what she saw there, and then she tore away her gaze and the dizzying feeling halted.

'Maybe I am in the wrong world.' She gave a soft laugh. 'Anyway, I need a date for the ball.' Now she blushed. 'I didn't mean…'

'I know you didn't, and as much as I would like to help with your predicament, for one thing I don't date and for another, tomorrow I return to my land.'

'Your land?' She frowned at his odd turn of phrase.

'Al-Zahir,' Rafiq said.

She nodded, deciding it was more polite than admitting…

'You've never heard of it.'

She gave a little laugh as he read her mind.

'It's close to Al-Nawar—have you heard of there?'

'No.' But then she thought for a moment. 'Maybe, they have a lot of rare flowers, don't they? I only know because we had some orchids flown in for a photo shoot.'

'That's the one. Well, Al-Zahir is more famous for its pearls and pearl diving, oh, and its desert.'

'It sounds beautiful,' she said, and would have asked

to hear more about it but the intercom crackled into life informing them they were at the end of the line.

'I've missed my stop,' Liliana yelped. 'By miles!'

'We've missed every stop.'

They had been so engrossed, so locked in conversation, the time had flown.

'It's the middle of nowhere.' She stood reading the timetable, and given they were way out of London, the tubes were not so regular.

'I know where we are,' Rafiq said. 'We're near Haven Manor—I went to an art viewing there a couple of years ago.'

Haven Manor was a gorgeous Jacobean manor that had once been the residence of a lord who had managed the surrounding land and tenant farms. Now it had been turned into a luxurious hotel and was also used for exclusive events.

Liliana knew it too.

'I've been too.' She nodded. 'I went there for a photo shoot, but we were mainly on the grounds. The old manor's beautiful.'

'Would you like to go now?' Rafiq suggested. 'We could have a drink, something to eat.'

'Oh!'

She must have looked so surprised or so shocked that he immediately moved to reassure her. 'Liliana, I didn't mean to cause alarm. I'm not asking you on a date or anything. I've already told you I don't do all that. I just…' He met her eyes then, and perhaps he too was a little surprised by things. 'I was enjoying talking to you.'

'And me,' she agreed and nodded and then gave him a nice smile. 'I'd love to go for a drink.'

Just a drink, mind—she certainly couldn't afford to eat there!

'It's a bit of a walk—I'll arrange a car.' It wasn't just the distance; Rafiq ought to let Salar know where he was. But then he thought of his security detail scrambling to get here and did not want the invasion and was thankful when she declined his suggestion.

'No need for that,' Liliana said. 'I just have to change my shoes.' She dived into her huge bag and held on to a bench as she switched her stilettoes to flats. 'Remind me to change them back before we go in.'

They were soon walking up a long lane with just the occasional vehicle swishing past and still they spoke, about nothing much at first, and then about so many things.

'Does your father have other children?'

She nodded. 'I've never met them though.'

'Would you like to?'

'No, and I'm quite sure they don't want anything to do with me. It all got rather messy. Do you have siblings?'

'A brother,' Rafiq said, and it properly dawned then that she didn't know him. Usually people he met, even for the first time, knew his status, but with Liliana he had a clean slate. He didn't have to reveal anything, yet so pleasant was the company, he did. 'Khalid. He died quite some time ago.'

'Oh,' she looked up. 'How old was he when he died?'

'Twenty-five.'

'I'm so sorry.' Liliana blinked. 'Were you close?'

People really didn't delve into his private life, not even lovers. His status or sometimes a glare was enough to hold them back, but Rafiq discharged neither bullet. 'I don't know,' he admitted. 'I thought we were close, but…'

When he didn't finish answering Liliana looked up, taking in his pensive features, wondering what had happened but choosing not to pry. 'You miss him?'

And from anyone else and on any other day, that question might annoy him but he stopped walking for a moment and so did she.

Her not knowing Khalid, and her lack of assumption helped.

Did he miss him?

For the first time he could almost separate the memory of his brother from Khalid's betrayal…

'Yes.'

Rafiq missed him dreadfully. He missed Khalid and his matter-of-fact ways. Missed texting him with his times when he completed a race. And he missed teasing him, because Khalid, who had been so unsentimental about the edicts and marriage, had fallen so deeply in love.

God, how he missed him.

It was why he'd headed out, why he'd been riding the tube, why he was now walking in drizzling rain just to forget…

First though, Rafiq knew, he had to remember.

CHAPTER THREE

IT WAS NICE to walk in the rain.

It was winter dark and the streetlights were on, and with no-one else around, it could have been midnight rather than just before six.

He asked if she still saw her father.

'No.' She shook her head as they walked side by side, her footsteps faster to keep up with his longer strides. 'I probably drove him away.'

'I'm sure that's not the case.'

'Oh, I was very annoying, I was so desperate to have time with him, just so eager and—' she thought of the best way to describe her rather needy younger self '—annoying.'

'No,' he refuted.

'Oh, yes.'

'I don't believe you.'

And Liliana did not know how to describe how she'd been so she decided to show him. Or was it that he'd seemed sad when he'd spoken of his brother and she simply wanted the return of his beautiful smile?

And so, from nowhere she took his hand, then with her other hand she took his arm and needily clung on, and sort of half skipped by his side.

Rafiq almost startled, but corrected himself so that he did not flinch, just glanced down with a frown, and there was Liliana looking up at him, her eyes wide and smiling.

'Liliana…'

'You said my full name!' She gazed up at him in wonder, then smiled so much her face must hurt and still she clung on, and in a sudden flash he realised he was seeing the little Liliana, and how she had once been.

'Stop.' He felt sad for her younger self and yet he was smiling, 'Liliana, stop,' he said as she continued to skip. 'Okay, you were annoying.'

'Told you!' she said and let go of him.

And then came a reward greater than his smile. He laughed, a low laugh, as gorgeous as distant thunder, and it was a real laugh, because for a second, he stopped walking.

He had never known anyone like her.

'You were also very cute,' Rafiq said and if he was not who he was, if there was even an inch in his life that allowed for casual, if this was another world, he would have put his arm around her and kissed the top of her head.

Instead, he looked ahead and they resumed walking.

'Almost there.'

Haven Manor really was as gorgeous as she remembered. 'It was summer when I was here,' she explained as they walked along a tree-lined driveway, dodging puddles. The rain had stopped and softly lit paths were all shiny, the magnificent building in the distance, but as of now they enjoyed a slow walk around the grounds.

'It's heavenly…' she sighed. It was all so tranquil. She could see the lights on in the mansion, even see some staff and people in the distance, but out here they were by themselves. 'I never really got a chance to explore. There's supposed to be a walled rose garden.'

'I don't think there'll be anything to see at this time of year,' Rafiq said, but it was still so nice to be alone together. It seemed neither were quite ready to go into Haven Manor and burst the bubble on their isolation—these moments that only contained them.

'Shall we take a look before we go in?' Rafiq suggested.

'Let's.'

They walked around the side of the grand building, following discreet signs, but given they were deep in winter the gate to the walled garden was padlocked shut.

'No roses for me,' Liliana said, jiggling the padlock and he saw that she pouted a touch.

Neither were ready yet to go in.

'We could walk around the lake?' Rafiq suggested.

Yes, it was cold, and were she here alone she'd surely shiver, but there was something so solid about him, as if his presence tamed the elements, or more that—just being here with Rafiq warmed her somewhere deep inside.

'Lucky you,' she said, thinking back to something he'd said about leaving tomorrow. 'Escaping the cold.'

For Rafiq there was no thought of tomorrow—it felt as if he'd already escaped.

There was a slight mist over the lake and they crossed a manicured lawn, then stood, simply taking it in.

'Were you here by day or night for your photo shoot?' he asked.

'By day,' she said looking up at a dark cloudy sky that

might be called dreary, but how could it be called that when you stood looking up at the sky with a man like Rafiq? 'You were here for an art viewing?'

'Yes.' He too thought back. For Rafiq it had been a short, formal visit as part of a packed schedule. Now though he noticed the details. He looked behind him and up to the little chimneys on top of the manor, then looked ahead at the dark shadows of the woodlands on the other side of the lake. Then he looked down at her. 'Though I don't recall it being as nice as this.'

'It is nice,' she admitted. 'I mean…' Liliana didn't know quite what she meant. 'This.'

'Yes.'

This was very nice.

'Why can't all first dates be as easy as this?' Liliana sighed and then was suddenly embarrassed by how that might sound. 'Not that this is a date!'

'It's not,' he affirmed. 'As I said, I don't date.' He seemed to think for a moment. 'I don't like entanglements.'

She nodded. 'And I think we both know you are way out of my league.'

He didn't, she noted, refute.

'And I'm not being all self-effacing or looking for compliments…' She looked up, knew that this man could have anyone; he was simply beyond anyone she'd seen, let alone met. And given her line of work she'd seen many beautiful people, but there was something intangible about Rafiq, something that held him separate from the rest. And then she thought of what he'd said about not dating. 'You're not married, are you?' she asked as they started to walk around the lake.

'God, no.'

'Involved with anyone?'

'I have lovers.' He did not add that since the kidnap, all his lovers had been security screened and cleared. There was nothing casual about Rafiq's life. 'But no-one has their heart turned to me…'

She'd gulped at his use of *lovers* in the plural, then frowned at his odd choice of words, then used them herself to ask a question. 'Is your heart turned to any of them?'

'No.' His response was immediate, and then he elaborated. 'It's made clear from the start that it is purely physical.'

'Purely?'

He gave a silent laugh at her nosiness. 'I don't…' He was about to say that he didn't date in the way she surely envisaged. That he was not one for romantic dinners, nor walks by a lakeside—that was not who he was. Except, here he was… 'My heart is incapable of turning.'

It was as cold as granite, just thumped at sixty beats a minute and mostly had since the hell of his capture. Exercise raised his heart rate, and sex did too, but little else. He'd been trained from childhood, but even the desert warriors who had taught him to hold emotions in check hadn't really envisaged that the skills might be put to such a brutal test.

Nine months of isolation, when his only contact had been the guards for beatings…

'I am not interested in relationships or love.'

'That's sad.'

'Not at all.' He shook his proud head. 'It is actually

quite reassuring—love exposes weakness, invites pain, allows for manipulation.'

He'd proved it.

They stopped walking and stood by the peaceful, still lake and somehow her presence let him remember.

'That smells good...'

Balach, the guard, ignored him; no doubt he thought the prisoner was angling for food.

But Rafiq wanted more than scraps.

Far more.

He wanted escape!

'Your wife must love you very much,' Rafiq persisted. 'She makes sure you are well fed.'

It was not a lie.

Some of his guards were hungry themselves, some came with bread or rice, yet Balach always came with a delicious home-cooked meal and coffee. For himself, of course. He spoke of his wife with affection to the other guards. Rafiq knew she was having a baby...

It was these things Rafiq noticed, storing away every minor detail, building a picture in his mind of all the guards.

Mean, cruel or just following orders...they changed often, but once a week or so, Balach appeared.

He was neither mean nor cruel and he did not simply follow orders, because one night Rafiq, in agony from a beating, had been returned to his cell. Balach had been there, only he hadn't replaced the chains so tightly that they bit into his flesh as the other guards did.

'Thank you,' Rafiq said.

Balach gave the smallest nod.

It told Rafiq his kindness had not been an accident.

* * *

'Oh.' A glint on the lake caught her eye. 'Swans…' she breathed. 'They must have been hiding.'

There were two, as pale as ghosts gliding on the still water.

'I'm very pleased to have missed my stop,' Liliana admitted as they stood watching the swans. 'If I hadn't, I'd be home now and all cross and upset.'

'That man really got to you.'

'Yes.' The air she sharply breathed out blew white. The anger that had propelled her from the café was clearly still there just beneath the surface. She glanced up to the man who stood quietly beside her, and there was something so reassuring about him, just this dignity to him that offered quiet comfort and made the recent hurt, which she would usually nurse alone, somehow possible to share. And yes, she could tell Rafiq what had been said. 'We'd barely got our coffees when he asked my body count…'

Rafiq frowned. 'Were you once in the military?'

'The military?' she repeated, a little lost by his response.

'Because that is not a question that should be asked.'

'The military…' She paused again, then realised what Rafiq meant. 'No…' She threw her head back and laughed. Gosh, how wrong could he get it? 'He wasn't asking how many people I'd killed in action. He meant…' Her laughter faded, the embarrassment stinging its way from her bruised heart to her flaming cheeks. 'He meant, how many…' She rolled her hand in explanation, waiting for realisation to hit. It didn't. His look still vaguely bemused. 'How many men I've…' Her breath hitched. 'I've slept with.'

Cross again, but not with him, she walked off, expecting him to join her, or not expecting anything. It was embarrassment that had her speeding off, but Rafiq caught her hand and halted her, turning her to face him. He would look her in the eyes when he gave his response.

'Then he's disgusting,' Rafiq told her. 'And you should have thrown your hand to his cheek rather than money to his table.'

'I abhor violence,' she said all pious and sweet, then added with a wry smile. 'More to the point, he might have slapped me back.'

'Don't meet up with men you don't know,' he warned her and then sighed at the contrariness of his own words. 'Says the man you don't know who has taken you to the middle of nowhere. However…'

'It's not the same.' Liliana said. 'We met…' She couldn't think of the word but Rafiq gave it to her.

'Naturally.'

'Yes.'

'You deserve better, Liliana.' Her heart skipped as it did when he used her full name. 'And you shouldn't have to be online looking for a date to avoid your manager.'

'I know,' she admitted.

'You have to make it clear that you're not into him.'

'I've tried. That's why I told him I'm seeing someone.'

'But you don't need an excuse.' He saw her sigh; knew it was too late for that. 'Do you have to go to this ball?'

'I do. I've made a few excuses to avoid Christmas functions.'

'Is it that bad?'

'It is,' she admitted. 'Unfortunately, our head of HR is his cousin.'

'Okay.' He wanted to arm her with defences. 'I'll tell you what to do.'

To use the little time they had, to give her all the tools.

He wanted to protect her and that was not a feeling he knew.

Rafiq decided he would give her a few tips, since he had a lot of experience closing down conversations and advances. However, it was a little hard to think when they were facing each other, so close that their white breaths mingled.

'You give them a look.'

'A look?' she echoed.

'To warn them, back off. Like this.' He snapped a warning glare at her, but clearly it didn't have its usual effect, because she laughed. 'You try it now.'

She did so.

Only it had no effect.

In fact, it had the reverse of the desired effect…

If anything, it accentuated desire.

'Okay,' he said brusquely. 'Suppose I ask you to dance, and you don't want to.'

'Don't be so ridiculous.' She smiled. 'I'd love to dance with you.'

She touched the lapel of his coat in a sort of playful thump.

And Rafiq was not used to playing, yet her hand on his chest, and the way it remained, felt sweet rather than cloying.

He wanted to capture her hand, or move her closer into him. He would like to touch the skin of her cheek, just to feel if it was as soft as it promised to be, or kiss that full mouth.

Instead, he stood there, feeling the touch of her hand on his chest, as light as a bird landing on your palm, but way, way more potent.

'Alright.' He would give this another go. 'Suppose I was to ask you the same question that that bastard did?'

'We've already established you wouldn't do that.'

'You're not making this easy,' he said. 'I am trying to give you a few pointers.'

'I know you are.' She pulled a serious face. 'Okay. Ask me again if I want to dance.'

She was thinking of more serious answers, yet her hand was still resting on his chest as she braced herself to respond more suitably.

'Liliana, would you give me the pleasure of this dance?'

Her face turned so red there must surely be steam coming from her cheeks and her voice was a squeak as she duly responded. 'No, thank you.' Oh, but she did; she wanted to lean on his chest and feel his arms wrapped around her, so badly she wanted to dance.

'What if I were to move in to kiss you?'

Liliana had not been expecting that, nor for the feel of his dark eyes moving down to her mouth.

'What then…?' he asked, his voice soft and low. His fingers moved a stray curl from her forehead and smoothed it behind her ear.

'Are you pretending to be my manager or that awful guy?' She could hardly breathe, let alone finish a sentence. To be so close, to feel his breath and inhale his scent and not respond was an impossible feat.

And he could feel the heat from her cheeks and her

hand was now gripping the lapel of his coat and he knew the effect he was having.

Could feel her effect on him too.

Rafiq had been born a flirt but that part of him had died a long time ago. Now he was too solemn, and anyway, it was unnecessary in his world. It was something though that came easily tonight, because he looked down at her plump mouth and grazed it just a little with his.

She moaned as he pulled his head back.

'Push me off,' he said, his lips hovering.

'I don't want to.'

'Slap my cheek,' he said as his shadowed jaw grazed her own. 'Knee me in the groin.'

She actually whimpered, shocked by her own thoughts for they dashed straight to his groin and it took two hands to grip the lapels of his coat now, just to stand up.

'I can't play this game with you,' she admitted. 'Because I want to dance and I want you to kiss me…' Oh, but she did. 'Please do.'

Kisses, if there were to be any, should surely come later, yet here they were right at the start of this night, and when he did as asked, she closed her eyes to the bliss, his kiss soft, gentle as if relishing her.

And relishing her he was.

Rafiq was not one for tender kisses by a lake, not one for sweet kisses that led nowhere. Yet tonight, he liked the labyrinth, the slight feeling of being lost, the thrill of discovery, because this gentle, slow kiss had her sigh, and he cupped her cheeks, parting her lips and sliding in his tongue.

Liliana had been kissed before.

At least she thought she had been, only nothing compared to this. She was pulling him closer, the kiss deepening, when usually it was Liliana pulling back. Usually, she was thanking her date for a lovely night and then fleeing. There was no thought of fleeing now; he was melting her with each stroke of his tongue.

All that seemed to exist was the feel of his mouth and strong warm body against her own.

With a will of their own her hands moved to his thick black hair and this was everything a kiss should be, everything she had never known.

It made her want more.

So much more.

And that startled her, enough that he must have sensed it because he pulled his head back a fraction.

'Okay?' Rafiq checked.

'Yes…' She nodded a little, and then more fervently, because she wasn't in the least upset by their kiss. More she was completely shocked at her own body's reaction. 'Yes, it's just…'

She knew she had to tell him, for that had been a kiss of lovers. Passion had poured from her, and she could feel him aroused against her stomach, feel her own body alive with an unfamiliar ache, and she rested her head on his chest. She had always felt safe with Rafiq but had never felt safer than now, being held in his arms, and she gazed at the swans and tried to fathom what was happening.

Finally, there was someone she could be honest with.

Completely.

'None,' she said. 'The answer to the question that guy asked is—none.'

CHAPTER FOUR

LILIANA EXPECTED RAFIQ to drop contact, or at least a slight startle as she effectively told him she was a virgin, but he remained still and continued to hold her.

Rafiq was silent. He was aware of his own distaste towards the man who had asked her such a crude question.

Certainly he did not want his response to be upsetting.

And, more to the point, that Liliana was a virgin should be irrelevant. He had not come here with any intention for bed. He had lovers, yes, but there were no one-night stands, no tumbling into bed with someone he'd only just met. There was nothing casual in any area of his life.

Their conversation, the walking, the embrace…all were uncharted territory.

He could feel her tense in his arms, even as she leaned against him, her head buried in his chest as if hiding, and he knew his reaction mattered.

'Come on,' Rafiq said. 'Let's go inside.'

She frowned. His response, or rather that he didn't dive in with questions, or make a comment, or even walk away, bemused her a little. Had Rafiq even heard or understood what she had just shared? She lifted her head and dared to look at him, her lips parting about to ask just that…but he looked down at her, and he gave her a small nod. His thoughts on the subject he did not share, but his direct gaze told her he had both heard and understood.

'Come on,' he said and started to walk towards the magnificent mansion.

'Rafiq,' she began as she caught up, 'What I told you, I just thought it important that you know, in case we…'

He looked over then. 'Did you think I brought you here for sex?'

'No.' She shook her head. When put like that it sounded too much, as if a couple of hours after they'd met they might have fallen into a hotel bed was too ridiculous to fathom. Yet when held in his arms, when lost in his kiss, it had felt obvious and utterly normal that they should extend that bliss 'No, I don't think that, but for the first time ever, when you kissed me…' She swallowed. 'I wanted more, but I thought you should know that I've never slept with anyone.'

'And now I do.' He gave her the smallest smile, and even though he gave her no answers, that smile calmed. Nothing she had revealed changed things. She glanced around as they walked and there seemed no record to the recent seismic shift—and for Liliana it was a seismic shift to have opened up so honestly to another. Yet the sky was still in place, the air still and cold as she turned and looked back to the swans, just resting.

The world was exactly as it had been before. Better even, for there seemed no awkwardness in regard to her untouched past.

'Perhaps change your shoes?'

'Pardon?' She blinked and then looked down and saw

her rather scruffy ballet flats and liked that one of them at least was thinking straight. ‘Oh, yes.’

This time as she changed her shoes she leaned on his arm to steady herself. Then side by side they walked towards the mansion but he did not take her hand. As they climbed the stone steps, she saw the doorman’s slight startle as he opened the door, and the concierge too seemed flummoxed as he looked over and saw the new arrivals. As if they hadn’t expected clients tonight.

Yet she could hear the murmur of conversation and laughter in the sumptuous cocktail lounge, and there were waiters walking with drinks and plates. Perhaps there was a private function taking place?

But no, the concierge was smiling now. ‘Your…’

Oh, the concierge was indeed flummoxed; it was not often royalty dropped in completely unannounced. Usually, if a VIP was about to suddenly descend then their secretary or security would give brief notice. As well as that there had been no vehicle to announce their arrival. He was an excellent concierge though and had recognised Rafiq from a visit a couple of years ago, but was damned if he could recall much more than that. Just as he had been about to say *Your Highness*, Rafiq had given him a look.

Rafiq, with that look, could halt an asteroid hurtling towards Earth, even reverse its course if he so chose.

And this look told the concierge that this very important guest did not want his title used and so he did not offer the visiting prince due recognition.

‘Welcome back, sir.’

Yes, an excellent concierge because he let Rafiq know that he remembered him.

'Thank you,' Rafiq responded. 'My guest is a little cold. I'd like a seat by the fire.'

'I don't think there are any,' Liliana said, peering in, but the concierge seemed to think it wouldn't be an issue.

'Of course, it will just take a moment.'

He really was the most helpful concierge, because he was sending someone off to clear a seat by the fire for them, and seemed concerned that it might take a moment to accommodate.

'May I take your coat, madam?'

'Yes, please,' Liliana said, 'and then I might go and freshen up.'

'Of course.'

And on this unexpected night, in which Rafiq had remained in control and together at each turn of events, it was as if more balls were suddenly thrown in for him to juggle.

As her trench coat slid off, Rafiq found he held his breath in his mouth, for summer had arrived on a winter's evening.

True summer.

The dress was a heavy cotton or linen, and white, yet dotted with flowers in every colour, poppies, forget-me-nots, buttercups, like a meadow. The skirt of the dress was flared and the top more fitted, the straps revealing bare, slender arms and scapulas. It was a dress for summer, yet even in the depths of winter it could never be considered out of place.

Even the concierge smiled. 'You have brought in the sun.'

'Thank you,' Liliana laughed.

Rafiq had known of her beauty, but not its extent.

Or rather, he was so unused to his own reaction, At the lake, what he'd said had been true; he'd brought her here with no intention of bed, yet right now, at this moment, he wanted to pick her up, tell the concierge to forget the fireside chairs and give them, now, this minute, a room.

He forced himself back to practical. 'What would you like to drink?'

'Tea,' she said, but then gave in, because not even three sugars were going to calm her down after that blissful kiss and her revelation. 'Actually, a brandy would be nice, but not…' She paused—really she didn't want to say here to not get anything too expensive. 'A brandy would be lovely.'

Even the loos were nice, and in a crimson wallpapered room, she stared into a huge mirror and yelped. Her hair was damp, wavy and wild and she smoothed it and then she took out her make-up bag and was about to do some major repair work on her flaming cheeks. But then she halted; Rafiq had already seen her.

He had seen her as she was.

Not just without the effect of the dress or the make-up; it went deeper than that. She had told him about her father, about her issues at work. She had told him so many things, even that she was a virgin.

And his reaction?

He had held her for a moment and then brought her in here.

Carried on as before.

It felt as if he knew her, possibly better than anyone in the world.

She settled just for some lip gloss and another quick

smooth of her hair and then headed out. A little nervous, a little excited.

A lot of things.

With a smile she walked towards the stranger who somehow knew her.

Rafiq had been shown to a seat by the fire, but shook his head when offered the menu.

Then he glanced over and saw a family. On the father's knee was a plump baby, smiling and playing with a coaster from the table.

He felt a clutch of fear, or was it more akin to terror? Guilt clawed at his scalp.

The baby looked at him. Smiled.

God, but why had he opened Pandora's box?

'Congratulations.' Rafiq said. He had heard the guards talking earlier and knew Balach had become a father. 'Did you have a boy or girl?'

Balach had not answered at first, but then he'd relented. 'A girl.'

'Lucky man,' Rafiq had said. 'Lur da kur jannat da...'*—a daughter is the paradise of the home.*

Balach had smiled to himself and carried on eating, but rather than clean his bowl with his bread as was usually the case he had brought it to Rafiq. 'Here,' he had said. 'It is not much.'

Rafiq knew that he was in.

Rafiq's heart had kicked into an uneasy thump as he thought of Balach and his baby, but then an English meadow caught his eye.

Usually heads turned when he entered—he was used to it—yet they turned tonight for the summery breeze she brought to the staid room.

Into his rather staid life.

Most would never consider his life as that; it was in fact spectacular, yet it was as if he viewed everything from a slight distance.

Not tonight.

He was immersed.

Liliana watched him stand as she approached and the flare of approval in his eyes had her stomach tighten in reflex as she walked towards him. He stood at a low table, and she took a seat in the fireside leather chair opposite him and then Rafiq did the same.

'You look beautiful,' Rafiq told her.

'So do you.'

His coat was off. That stunning suit she could examine properly now, but instead she found herself a little nervous to look over to him, let alone meet his eyes.

A waiter came with their drinks and some odd contraption he was ready to light if she preferred her cognac warmed.

'I'm fine,' she politely declined, really a little worried about money now, especially when he asked if they would like anything else. 'No, thank you,' Liliana rather hurriedly said. 'We're not eating.'

Instead of the contraption, Rafiq warmed the cognac in his palm for a couple of moments as Liliana tried to take in her surrounds, wanting to later recall every detail. She could only think of Rafiq though.

There was something deferential in the way the staff

treated Rafiq. Despite having no booking they'd sat fireside, with a waiter discreetly hovering but clearly there just for them. For him.

She had been here with work, admittedly most of her time had been spent in the grounds, but there had been a sumptuous lunch. She thought of the director, Matthew, clicking his manicured fingers and tutting at the slightest delay. How Kasia, the model, had moaned about the seating or an olive, or something she wanted changed, and the staff had been more than accommodating.

Yet for Rafiq, there was a subtle difference…and she tried to place quite what it was. He didn't, like the executives in her company and the models who had been there that day, demand the best. To Rafiq the best was readily given.

She frowned, trying to understand her own thoughts, and what they meant and suddenly shy, she looked over to him.

'Here.' He handed over her glass, warmed by his palm.

'Thank you.' She took a sip of her drink. 'Gosh, that's far too nice.' She decided to address the dreaded money issue. 'Just the one though. I can't afford to be going Dutch too many times in one night.'

'Dutch?' He frowned but then remembered back from his student days, when life had been lighter and bills would be shared. And though she smiled and made light, he did not forget she had recently had to walk out on a truly terrible date.

'Liliana,' he said. 'Tonight I shall be paying for things, and I shan't hear otherwise…' Her mouth opened to protest, and then she blushed a little. 'And may I assure you that if at any time you feel uncomfortable…' He paused, realising that words were perhaps not enough, and so he signalled to the waiter and asked for the concierge to be brought over.

'Can I know your surname?' Rafiq asked her.

'Hamilton,' Liliana said and then the concierge appeared.

'Miss Hamilton might have to leave at short notice—can you please ensure a car is ready for her?'

'Of course.' The concierge nodded.

When they were alone, he gave her a grim smile. 'At any time, all you have to do is request your driver.'

'Thank you,' she said, thinking how kind he was to think of that, especially after what she had just told him. 'I mean that. It's very thoughtful of you.'

'So,' he said, 'tell me about this dress I won't see…'

And she was no longer shy. 'When you *don't* take me to the ball,' she sweetly smiled.

'I really cannot.'

'I know. I was just teasing.' She actually tapped his foot with her own. 'The dress is heaven. Though, if I'm honest…'

'You're not honest though,' he teased and tapped her foot back.

'I can be.'

God, they were sitting respectfully apart, yet devouring each other with their eyes, and there was a penalty shootout taking place beneath the table. Not quite, just the odd tap but this was more than mere conversation. It was sublime.

'If I tell you something you must promise never to share it.'

'Of course,' he agreed and politely nodded.

'The company I work for,' she said and winced for a second. 'I don't like a lot of their designs.'

He waited and when she didn't elaborate, he frowned. 'That's it?'

'I feel disloyal even saying it. They tend to do too much, go over the top at the last minute and add too much detail. But this dress I've bought.' She dived into her bag and took out a huge sketch pad, flicking the pages. 'It's couture, but the client changed her mind during the fittings, and so it was never finished off, but that actually suits me, no extra frills. I did a quick sketch.'

He sat there as she handed it across the table.

It took all his effort to take the pad rather than move their chairs closer—he wanted to feel her head by his as he surveyed her work, yet he was supremely polite and held out his hand.

She handed him the pad, and their fingers brushed, their eyes meeting, and he saw her look of slight bemusement that a mere touch of fingers could make you ache, but he remained stoic and withdrew his gaze and looked down to the page.

A quick sketch!

It was a work of art in itself.

'May I?' he asked, lifting up a page, to check if she minded him looking through her work. And when she nodded, he found he smiled when he recognised one of her sketches. He looked over to where she sat, blushing a little as he surveyed her designs and then handed the pad back to her. 'You *made* the dress you are wearing?'

'Yes.'

'Then you are very talented.'

'I wish someone would tell my boss.'

'Have you thought about doing your own work, starting out by yourself?'

'Of course I have,' Liliana said, 'It's the dream. I do make a few things now and then and sell them but I don't want to end up doing alterations and such…' He gave her a quizzical look that invited her to explain further. 'The plan is to put together an upmarket off-the-peg collection and then rent the tiniest shop.' She sighed. 'I don't know if you can see from those sketches but the fabrics that I love are really expensive.'

'I can tell that from the dress you are wearing.'

'Actually, for this one I found the fabric in a thrift store in Marylebone. I think it might have started life as a tablecloth.'

His eyes took in the fabric, and then his gaze moved to her shoulders, and down the length of her pinkening arms, and then slowly back up, dusting her shoulders and to her burning face.

It felt as if he'd just stroked her, or kissed up her arm.

'What colour is your new gown?' he asked, handing her back the pad.

'Pink.' Then she hurriedly added, 'Now, pink can be problematic…'

'I agree.'

She glanced up, a little surprised by his reaction. 'Not with your complexion.' His caramel skin could wear it well.

'Not to wear—I meant I have a pink horse and he is indeed problematic.'

'Sorry?' She must have misunderstood.

'Well, he is rose gold—he's an Akhal-Teke.' She clearly had not heard of the rare breed. 'Their coat has a metallic sheen in certain lights. I have them in several shades. Gold, silver, a beautiful copper…my stallion is rose gold.'

'I don't believe you.' She smiled and sipped her drink, certain he was teasing her again, but there was no tap of his foot to confirm that he was. No private smile.

'But it's true.' He took out his phone and swiped through, and then handed it to her.

The same brush of fingers and when she looked at his stunning horse and her mouth gaped, he could resist no more. Possibly, to the waiter's and hovering concierge's horror, their surprise guest, a crown prince no less, got up and moved his chair for himself.

Liliana almost closed her eyes in relief as Rafiq positioned his chair beside her own so that they sat together. She could feel his thigh on hers and their arms touching again as he swiped through.

'He's beautiful.'

'He knows it,' Rafiq said, showing her more images. Only Liliana could barely take in the magical horse; more, she was noticing the very solid long thighs of the rider wearing jodhpurs, and those long forearms and the hands that loosely held the reins… Then she saw a dark shadow on his wrists and frowned, but there wasn't time to properly examine the image or zoom in as he had already swiped on.

And her breath caught again, for he was galloping on sand and wearing black robes. 'Where's that?'

'Al-Zahir's desert.'

'Wow!' The contrast between the blue skies and golden sands was so vivid but again she was looking mainly at the rider.

Rafiq, of course, spoke about his horse. 'That is around midday. You can't really see the sheen there—I'll find one at sunrise. We call it the golden hour for these horses, because the slant of light brings out the colours and metallic sheen.'

They were lost in time again, as they had been on the tube, but there was so much more between them now.

Oh, this man changed and surprised at every turn, and she felt almost dizzy from her own shallow breathing. But as he swiped again, she looked not at the images but down to his wrist, which was now exposed a little by the cuff of his shirt and she wasn't sure if it was a dark tattoo or…a scar?

He must have felt her stare. 'Don't ask,' Rafiq told her in a low voice, and she nodded, accepting the instruction not to mention it.

'Okay.' Then she gave up on horses and turned her head so that all that remained in the world was his eyes. 'I know why I told you I haven't slept with anyone.' She had made up her mind at their first kiss, before that even. 'Will you be with me tonight?'

He didn't blink—her request was clearly not a complete surprise. The air was electric between them, molecules leaping and colliding as her body silently begged him not to deny her and Rafiq attempted to resist.

'You deserve so much more than a one-night stand for your first time.'

'I disagree.' She shook her head slowly. 'I expected it to be so much less.'

'Liliana,' he reminded. 'I leave tomorrow.'

'I know that.'

'I'm not sure you do. I would love to say that when I

return, I shall wine and dine you, take you to the ball, but that would be a lie.'

'I know that too.'

'Do you? The thing is, I am…'

Liliana knew there was about to be a disclosure—he was about to give her the reason they could never ever work and, quite simply, she did not want to hear it. She didn't want to think about impossible futures, just knew she did not want this fantasy night to end.

'Don't say it.'

She gently placed her fingers to his lips. Whatever it was, she didn't want or need to know, and he captured her hand for a moment, and she willed him to kiss it.

He did not.

There could be no public displays for a man in his position.

Yet he was glad she had stopped him, for he didn't want to reveal his title or his past. Nor did he want to reveal his jaded and bitter self.

He could though be the person she needed tonight.

Just for one night.

Gently he removed her hand.

'Not here,' he said, 'we cannot touch here.'

The old Liliana might have taken that as a rejection, but Rafiq brought out the new. A braver new, a bolder new.

'Then take me somewhere we can.'

CHAPTER FIVE

LILIANA LEFT ALL details to Rafiq.

There was no room in her mind to fathom the hows and whys, but even the short time it took for him to arrange for them to be alone felt far too long.

But soon an escort had invited them to please follow him to their suite. While he led them up the carpeted stairs they walked together, though not holding hands.

They were taken up another flight of stairs and turned towards a secluded wing in the grand old mansion.

Rafiq didn't dismiss their escort as such, but subtly let him know he wanted no more intrusion. With a polite "thank you" that said he would manage the door himself, Rafiq took the key and their escort melted away.

She stepped into a room that glowed amber from the light in a colossal stone fireplace dominating one wall. Then her eyes were drawn to the huge four-poster bed that anchored the room, draped in scarlet-and-gold linens. She looked up to the wooden-beamed ceiling and around the magnificent suite—to the chaise longue beneath the window and then back to the roaring fire that seemed to leap with the same primal energy that danced between them…

Rafiq too was checking the room. He left her for a

brief moment and went to pour some spiced wine from a decanter, but she shook her head so he placed it back down. Then he headed to the heavy oak bedside table, sliding open the drawer, and the silver-foil-wrapped condoms seemed too modern for this ancient place.

For Rafiq even?

The palace usually took care of such details. Tonight, the brand-named packages seemed a little crude compared to the bespoke gold-foil wrappers he was more used to.

This night went against all instructions, all logical knowings and serious edicts.

Then he looked over to where she stood, shivering in the warm room, as if alone without his touch, and this night was the most vital, the most imperative he had known.

'Come here,' he told her and she stumbled towards him.

'I am nervous,' she admitted, 'But please, I want you so much.'

'I know. You can tell me you're nervous.'

'Yes.'

She felt as if she could tell him anything. Ask for anything. 'Kiss me.'

He obliged, toying with her mouth, until the goosebumps had gone from arms that now coiled around him.

She adored his kiss and the stealth of his warm fingers and she was so happy she'd designed such a simple dress as it slipped off, and then he pulled back a little, admiring her jade lacy underwear.

'You are perfection…' he told her, stroking her pert breasts until her nipples thickened and ached beneath the lace. Then he took off her bra and his touch was light on her pale breasts, and then with the back of his hand, stroked down her stomach.

There was nothing shy about them, just tenderness and want. Both discovering her together. He liked how she moaned as he slipped his hand into her knickers and stroked her, how she writhed a little as he added to the bliss with deep kisses to her neck. And Liliana liked how he then slowly peeled off her knickers, how he knelt and admired her, fluffing the flame of pubic hair, admiring her golden curls and then kissing her there.

'Oh, God,' she said, wishing she wasn't suddenly so unsteady in stilettoes. So intense was the pleasure as he parted her intimate lips and kissed her there, she was holding his head just to stay upright.

'Stay there,' he ordered in a ragged voice and as his tongue flicked her tenderly, he slipped his hand between tense thighs and explored her intimate lips with both his mouth and his fingers.

'Rafiq...' She was already in bliss, or on the edge of this rush of craving, for she stood naked in her shoes and was being softly devoured and tenderly stroked. 'I want to...' She didn't quite know what she wanted, or quite how she was feeling, but she was tensing to his touch, holding on to his wide shoulders as her thighs started shaking...

The moment they had met she had told him she was more than capable of standing.

She was close to incapable now.

As he rose to his feet she impatiently tugged at his jacket, wanted him naked and for their skin to know each other.

Rafiq read her wants and soon that divine suit had dropped to the floor. When even the mere thought of sex had made her a little anxious before, being with him felt as natural as breathing. His chest was wide and with a fan of black hair and she was clumsily trying to kiss his dark mahogany nipples as he dealt with the bottom half of his clothes… And then they were naked, warm and deeply kissing, his manhood between them, and she could stand for not a moment more.

Rafiq turned to push further back the covers on the downturned bed and her breath caught when she saw the scars on his back, jagged and vicious.

No, the mark on his wrist was not a tattoo—indeed they were scars, for they were on both wrists and his ankles too.

Rafiq turning his back was deliberate.

He did not want to see her shock, and no masseuse or lover of his would dare inquire. Back home they knew; here they knew better than to comment.

Rafiq was about to turn back to face her and to get back to kissing her as if to erase from her mind what she'd just seen, but then her fingers came to his back and gently acknowledged the darkened, thick scars.

It was the first true tenderness he had allowed.

A light dust of her fingers, and there was comfort in her touch that he allowed for just a brief moment before turning around, and they stared in silence.

And he had never been more grateful that she did not ask for details, but there were tears in her eyes.

'I'm so sorry,' she said, for whatever had happened.

'It's okay,' he assured, and then told her something that felt important. 'I'm okay.'

'Good.'

That was it.

The hurt acknowledged.

And nothing outside them mattered. They were on the sumptuous bed, side on and kissing and licking and exploring each other. His mouth on her breasts, his erection nudging her thigh and her untutored hand crept down to his…

'I really should be scared.' She gave a soft laugh, and they both knew she referred to his impressive length, 'Why aren't I scared, Rafiq?'

'Because this is…' He did not know.

They were stripped of more than their clothes; they were baring themselves, and there were no titles or rules in this bed, no touch denied.

He trapped her in his legs, and she kissed his chest, her teeth nipping, moving up to his neck and inhaling him. Then the tighter trap of his legs turned her like a death roll and she lay breathless on her back. Rafiq spread her legs with his knees, and knelt between them and stared down at her.

As if considering.

'Please,' she said, and lifted her head to aim for his mouth, but he knelt up and reached for a condom.

Rafiq had indeed been considering.

God knows he wanted to feel her with his naked length, and seeing her willing eyes, her pleas, it took the last grains of common sense to reach for a condom.

Rafiq came over her, kissed her again, felt her hot body eager for his.

He had *never* made love like this.

Never before.

Not like this—there was eye contact, kissing, tenderness and assurances as he nudged into her tight space.

'Oh, God…' She was both in pain and in heaven as he nudged into her, biting the salty skin of his shoulder. He liked the nip of her teeth, and how raw they were together. How much of each other both wanted.

'Ow…' she said and regretted it, for she could feel him holding back, trying to be gentle as he filled her. Even gently there was a moment of agony as he tore into virgin flesh and then she no longer was, for he was moving inside her.

Liliana felt as if they were one, as if they were moving together, but more, sharing their bodies, giving and receiving, but always giving…giving her kiss, giving her hips up to meet his, just giving as he too gave, a deeper thrust, then moving onto his elbows, as if he knew the very second the crush of his large body became too much.

Giving her more pleasure and she did not know what this was—it couldn't be love, but it felt like possession, as if this night she was absolutely his. And then he perhaps felt the same, because the thrusting slowed, though it was very deep and intimate as he looked into her eyes.

'You say,' he said as he kissed her parted mouth, drank her hot breath between words. 'If he asks you to…' He closed his mind in distaste, not wanting to think of her manager in the moment, or of visions of her being asked by another to dance, but he said it with reason. He gave her the words to say when he could not be there to intervene: 'Rafiq would not like it.'

The room went black, the amber gone, as if the fire had leaped from the fireplace to their centres, and he thrust into her. He gave a shout and she shattered beneath him, tightening as he released into her. Her intimate space felt as if it gave aching kisses back. She was, Liliana was sure as she came back to amber light, a hot, sweaty mess beneath him, but he looked at her with eyes that adored.

And she was already dreading the morning.

For she felt the turn of her heart.

CHAPTER SIX

Liliana was determined not to sleep.

She wanted every second of this wonderful night, but lying in his arms in their red-and-gold bed, her head resting on his chest, felt like sedation. Their bodies were warm, identically so, and the feel of him stroking her hair or her arm as they sleepily spoke was idyllic.

They spoke about her all-girls school versus his private one. How she was so awkward with people. Chatty, but deep down shy.

'Why did you wait?' he asked.

'Because…' She lay there, an answer on the tip of her tongue, but she swallowed it back.

I think I was waiting for you.

Too needy?

Too much?

But the truth.

'Because…?' he prompted.

'I don't know,' she finally answered. 'I guess I'm not very used to boys or men. School was all girls, and there was just my mum…'

'Does she have a partner?'

'No.' She shook her head. 'I think she'd drop everything for him, even now.' She thought back. 'His wife found out.'

She liked that he remained silent. There was just the stroke of his hand on her arm, or sometimes he toyed with her hair.

'I was about seven or eight and there was a knock at the door. I thought it was a friend wanting to play. Instead, it was this angry-looking lady. It was awful,' she admitted. 'I ran up to my room and hid…' She gave a low laugh. 'I hate confrontation.'

'She wasn't cross with you, surely?' Then he was silent and lifted her chin so she looked up. 'Did she know about you?'

'Not until then. I have my father's colouring.' She thought back to that awful day, and the terrible things that had been said about her very existence. 'I'd always felt like the odd one out, but that day made it so much worse. I heard my mum say I was an accident, and his wife saying her children would always come first.'

It was so calm being in his arms. She could tell him about that terrible time and somehow his touch took the sting out of her shame.

'After that, he used to come down now and then, but not…' She felt tears sting her eyes and not even the balm of his embrace could take away the pain of this memory. 'Just not to see me. I worked it out when I was eleven or so that he'd never really been there to see me.'

'How?'

He wanted, Liliana realised, to hear it. To hear her. 'We got let out of school early, and I came home and they were sitting having a coffee… I was thrilled to see him,

I always was. I just assumed he was here for dinner, but then he looked at the time and said he had to go.' She sniffed, but knew a tear had dropped onto his chest and hoped he didn't know. 'I realised he'd come to see my mother, that he hadn't expected me to be home.'

'You're sure?'

'Yes, it was obvious once I knew. There were plates in the kitchen, they must have had lunch. I realised then that he didn't think of me as his family. He'd just come to see my mum. I think they saw each other a lot more than I knew… It really hurt.'

'I bet.'

'I'd got it in my head that he couldn't get away much, because of his work and such…' She had made up so many excuses for him. 'Delivering foals and things.'

'Kitten emergencies,' Rafiq said, and she smiled because she had told him about the lies she'd told to keep the fantasy of having a family intact.

'I didn't have anything to do with him after that.'

He squeezed her bare arm and she felt better for having told another, truly. 'So, what was your worst day?' she asked sleepily and then winced. 'Oh, God.' She sat up; he had said not to ask about it. 'Rafiq, I really am sorry, I just forgot about your scars.' She really had. 'Does that make me selfish?'

'No.' He smiled. 'It's very nice that you forgot about them.' It really was and he pulled her back into his embrace. 'Anyway, that wasn't the worst…' There had been many beatings, many days of torture, but there wasn't one he could separate. They had all been their own version of hell.

* * *

'Still your father refuses to help you...' The guards continued with their taunts.

Rafiq stared ahead.

'All he has to do is withdraw his support for the King of Al-Nawar.'

Rafiq knew his father would never back down and while it hurt, while he felt forgotten, he refused to show it.

'Your family thinks little of you...'

He would rather the lash of the whip than the verbal taunts, but not once did he let them know that.

'Your father would lose his own sons for a country that isn't even his own.'

That hurt.

His father would support the uprising in Al-Nawar rather than negotiate to free his sons, but again, Rafiq refused to react.

'And your brother gave you up.'

That sideswiped him a touch. 'Hichvaght!' *Rafiq had even given a sneering smile as he'd refuted—Never!*

'Of course he did. How do you think we got into your home? How else could we know about the tunnel?'

'Hichvaght!' *Rafiq had said again, but perhaps with less certainty. For a second it was as if part of his soul left his body, or something tore in his heart. 'Khalid would never.'*

The fire was dying and he should get up and throw on a log, but instead he stared at the ceiling, stroking her hair. And he would never see her again. He could admit things he never could in his real life. This night was just about them, and so he told her one of his worst days. 'My brother betrayed me.'

Liliana went to sit up again. She honestly hadn't expected him to tell her anything and had been secretly kicking herself for being insensitive about his scars, but he pulled her down to his chest.

'What happ—' She stopped talking, remembering how gentle it had felt when he hadn't asked questions or delved, just let her tell him what she wanted.

'I don't talk about it, even with my family. It feels disloyal to his memory,' he said. 'I think deep down, they know what he did. My father cannot look at me, we cannot talk about him.'

Liliana frowned, wishing he would tell her what had happened, but knowing it wasn't her place to ask.

'I don't want to talk about it,' Rafiq said, but not unkindly.

Nor did he want to expose her to his colder, distant self. Saying his brother had betrayed him out loud had hollowed him. He had already admitted more than he ever had, and it felt odd to have voiced the truth that had been in his head for fourteen years.

Khalid *had* betrayed him. He had told the guards a secret only they and their father knew. And yes, they must have put him through hell; Rafiq was in no doubt as to that. But there was another thing he was certain of—he would never have told his captors about the tunnel, never would he have given them access to his brother.

Hichvaght.

Never.

He slid her up his body, lowered his head and closed that topic with a kiss that led them back to heaven.

They made love through the night and they shared parts of themselves that they wanted to.

And while he did not tell her more about Khalid, or how he'd received the scars, he did share other things. Things he'd long since stopped thinking about… He wasn't even sure how this forgotten piece of him came up.

'You were a sprinter?'

'Ages ago,' he said and nodded. 'When I was at university.'

'Did you do hurdles?' she asked. 'I hated them at school.'

His chest lifted in a silent laugh. 'No, no hurdles.'

'Did you have a favourite?'

He thought back. 'The four hundred metres…' He breathed in deeply, just recalling the velocity and speed and the sheer exhilaration. 'I only did it up till twenty-one though.'

'Most people give up after school.'

'No, I loved it.

'So, you were a serious sprinter.'

'For a while.'

'How come you stopped?'

'Just…' He breathed in. 'I lost form. I guess life got in the way.'

'When your brother died?'

His hand stopped mid-stroke of her arm. 'You're very observant.'

'I am.' She smiled and felt his chest hairs tickling her cheek. It was so nice lying here talking. It really had been the most wonderful night. 'What time is your flight?'

'I have to leave here around seven.'

There was no clock she could see and Liliana did not want to delve for her phone. It didn't matter anyway; whatever time it was now, was too close to the end of them.

'What will you do today?' Rafiq asked.

'Sleep,' she said, only that wasn't an honest answer and she sat up and looked at him. 'I can't hide from you, Rafiq.'

'I don't want you to hide.'

And so, she answered him honestly. 'I'll probably go home and cry my eyes out,' Liliana admitted. 'And then sleep, and then…' He was stroking her breast. 'I don't know, I've never done any of this before.' Not just the sex, but the feeling of being so close to another. 'I've got a confession.'

'You're hungry?'

'I am,' Liliana said, 'but it's not that.'

'Tell me.'

'On the tube…'

'Yes?'

'I think I knew I'd missed my stop.'

He smiled. 'You think?'

'Okay, I knew.'

'I didn't have a stop in mind, but I chose not to look up too.'

'Really?'

'I think we were just enjoying each other too much for it to end.'

It had to end though.

For Rafiq, this was unsustainable. Already she felt a little too close to his heart, and that was somewhere he didn't want another to be. Even if he hadn't shared the details, he couldn't quite believe he had told her about Khalid's betrayal.

He regretted telling her, in fact.

Liliana had no regrets.

He made love to her again, and then they shared breakfast in bed, feeding each other between kisses, and there was nothing she would change about this night.

One thing.

There would be no morning.

CHAPTER SEVEN

Both Liliana and Rafiq hated that morning.

'We'll say goodbye here,' Rafiq had told her.

His hair was wet from the shower, and his suit was as divine as it had been on first sight. Apart from being unshaven he looked as together as he had when they'd first met.

'You're better at this than me,' Liliana said as she sat up in bed and a couple of tears escaped when she'd sworn she wouldn't cry. Of course he was better at this than her; after all he chose not to have relationships or entanglements.

She'd known that when she'd asked him to take her to bed. Only she hadn't known then just how badly it would hurt watching him pull on his coat and knowing this was a forever goodbye.

'Call down to reception when you're ready for the driver.'

'I will.'

'Have him take you home.'

'I'll get the tube.'

'Let me do this for you. If I wasn't getting a plane, I'd ensure you got home.'

'Okay.'

'And no crying,' he said. 'Have a sleep instead.'

'I might do that.' She attempted a smile. 'Who are you flying with? I can see when you take off…' She pulled a face. 'That sounds a bit stalkerish.'

'Tracking my flight?' He smiled as he came over for a final kiss goodbye. 'It does a bit.'

His kiss was light, not like the deeply intimate ones they'd shared last night. And it had to be that, because despite appearances, Rafiq was struggling not to reach for his phone. With one call he could delay his flight, shrug off his coat and climb back into bed.

But instead of doing that he brushed her lips with his and tried not to notice how naked and warm and willing she was.

So willing. His light kiss wasn't enough. Liliana wanted more and so she rose up onto her knees and her arms lifted to reach for him, but he abruptly lifted his head.

It felt as if she'd been slightly told off or rather warned to stay back.

But then he relented and, lowering his head, his mouth found hers again. His kiss soft and deep, then wet and warm…and her hands were back up and holding his head and she was a touch breathless when he released her.

'I'll go.'

'Yes.'

She kept in the tears, and even managed a little wave as he left and he was proud of her for doing so, because this goodbye had been hard.

Once out the door he leaned against the wall for a moment. '*La'nat, la'nat…*' he cussed at his own weakness.

Even away from her, with a solid door between them, he was fighting not to go back.

The taste of her kiss was still on his lips but he wiped it off with the back of his hand then took the stairs down. And in case she was watching, he refused to look up or back as he walked to the waiting vehicle.

Salar's face was grim, given the man he should be guarding had been out all night.

'Sir,' he greeted, holding the car door open.

And when they were in the car.

'Sir, if you can please just let me know…'

His voice faded as Rafiq closed the privacy screen.

Back to his self.

His bastard self.

'I am sorry to hear about your brother,' Balach said. 'Peace be upon him.'

The other worst day of his life.

Had it been any of the other guards Rafiq would have spat—they had killed Khalid after all—but he knew the sympathy that Balach offered was genuine.

Balach was a good man.

And of course, Rafiq knew that with Khalid dead it was more imperative than ever that he got out.

His body was wasting away, his soul crushed with loss and bewildered at his brother's betrayal, but he pushed all thought of that aside and focused on what he must.

Balach had been quiet these past weeks.

Later he had started his dinner, but it was just bread and the scents were not as tantalising, even to a starving man.

There was something wrong at home, Rafiq was sure.

As the night crept on, Rafiq looked over at the hunched figure, scooping sand and running it through his hand, and knew something was deeply troubling Balach.

'How's your baby?'

Balach did not respond.

'Your daughter, she must be eight weeks old now...'

Still Balach said nothing.

'Your wife must miss you on these long nights,' Rafiq said a while later, willing Balach to respond, and to find out what was wrong.

'She is worried.' Balach had turned his head slightly.

'Oh.'

'The baby is not well.'

'I am so sorry to hear that.'

Balach had nodded.

'Is it serious?'

'Her heart...' Balach said. 'She needs surgery.'

'There is a lot that can be done these days.'

'For you perhaps...' Balach sneered.

Liliana had entered so willingly into one night.

So why did her heart ache with grief as she kissed him goodbye forever?

And why did her mind silently scream when the promised car took her to her door?

And why had she been so angry when a few days later a woman had arrived with a case? Liliana, her eyes swollen from crying had been about to close the door on the elegant woman, but she had said she was here on behalf of Rafiq.

Liliana had been offered to select a gift, and she stared at the baubles and any one of them might solve every problem, her financial ones at least, but her mouth had twisted in distaste.

'Tell Rafiq—I am insulted.'

So insulted.

It had been nice to huff and puff and stay angry for a couple more weeks but then there had been another knock on the door to her little flat and she had a delivery.

A massive delivery. Two men carried in ream after ream of fabric, all covered in a protective layer of muslin, and she showed them to her study.

And this gift was not an insult…

Velvets, silks, damasks and cashmere, in soft colours and golden sheens, and she even gasped when her fingers brushed vicuña, the most coveted of fabrics, the very softest of wools.

The tears fell then for she knew what this meant. She could start to build her own business. Only she knelt on the floor and wept on silk, hating that the future he was helping her with would be without him.

Three months later

As Liliana herself had predicted, all too soon the skies were blue and the dress was pink.

A very pale blush pink in the softest organza, the hand-stitched pleats brought out a little more bust than she'd thought she had. The skirt fell in more soft pleats, and usually she'd be beyond excited and twirling in the mirror, but nothing felt quite as good as it had before Rafiq…

It had been three months since they had shared the night and her heart still ached as if it were yesterday.

'Gordon and James are going to keep an eye,' Margo told her as they sat at dressing tables and touched up their make-up in the ladies' rooms. 'If Simon makes an approach, one of them will drag you off to dance, or I'll dash you off back here.'

'I'll be fine,' Liliana said, but even if the Simon problem had shrunk in proportion since losing Rafiq, it was nice that she had colleagues looking out for her. 'Thanks though.'

'It's a shame he couldn't be here,' Margo added.

'Who?'

'Oh, I would love to know who.' Margo smiled. 'One day you'll tell me.'

Liliana doubted it.

She didn't even know how to explain that magical night to herself. How she'd simply lost herself to Rafiq, how she'd told him things she'd never shared with another, how they'd met and a mere matter of hours later she'd asked him to take her to bed.

How did she convey that the hours with him had been the happiest of her life, as if somehow their souls had recognised each other?

If she ever told someone and then added that he'd tried to pay her in precious gemstones they'd think she'd simply been bought.

She must have stood up a little too abruptly, because she felt the teeniest bit dizzy and had to hold on to the dressing table for a moment.

'You're fine,' she scolded herself, deciding she hadn't eaten enough in the excitement of getting ready for the ball.

Only she didn't feel excited.

She was starting to get seriously worried, and telling herself there was no need to be. After all he had used protection as they'd made love over and over that night.

It was just something she'd been expecting still hadn't happened.

And her breasts were definitely bigger.

The drinks were flowing and not for the first time in recent weeks, she declined.

And then near the end of the night, when she'd ducked and dived to avoid Simon, she was too busy daydreaming about Rafiq and worrying about late periods to notice that the dreaded moment had arrived.

'Watch out,' Margo warned as Simon made his way over, but the warning came too late for Margo to whisk her off or Liliana to subtly disappear.

'Lili? Finally. Would you…?'

She knew what was coming—of course she did—and she even had her emergency line ready: *Rafiq would not like it*. But when she thought of that deeply intimate moment, her body beneath him, the snap of possession in his voice, she knew she would not be able to say those words without weeping. And she wasn't going to share any of that precious night with anyone. Certainly not Simon.

'I…'

That was all she managed to get out, for if she'd felt a little dizzy before, she felt as if she was on a carousel as Rafiq called out her name.

'Liliana.'

The chandeliers must have exploded, or something just as spectacular, because her mind was struggling to process what was happening when she heard Rafiq's beautiful deep voice.

'I'm unforgivably late.'

He didn't kiss her but as he joined her at her side, he slid his hand around her waist and looked at Simon, who simply shrivelled and stepped back.

'Rafiq.' She almost drooped in relief that he was near again, and with a slight stumble was straight to his arms, and he took her to the dance floor.

'I never dreamed…' She was almost crying.

'I know.'

Rafiq did know.

God knows he had done all he could to stay away, but her refusal of his first gift, the acceptance of the second, the endless thoughts of her…

Yara had been right to warn him; the pressure for them to marry was intensifying. And though Rafiq was standing his ground, he knew the demands would not relent.

This morning, he had woken with dread…

His life really was a succession of anniversaries.

Today was the national day of mourning for Khalid.

And knowing where Liliana was tonight had proved too much and after dealing with formalities he had summoned the royal jet.

He had landed too late to escort her, though he was here to offer far more than that.

At least it had meant he'd avoided the cameras and attention of the red carpet, for this reunion should not be taking place in public.

For Rafiq *this* was extremely reckless.

His intention had been to arrive and gesture his head for her to join him, then leave. Then he had seen Liliana, the sketch of the dress come to life, and that man walking over to ask her to dance…

Indeed, Rafiq did not like what he was seeing—he knew on sight that this was the man Liliana had been referring to.

And so, he had slid a hand possessively around her waist and contact had been made, and then how could he not ask her to dance the last dance?

Their first, but also his.

She could not know this was strictly forbidden.

The music was slow and dreamy, and she wanted to sink into his arms and rest her head on his chest, but he held her very formally.

'Later…' he said, pulling her apart from him just a little. 'When we are alone.'

He could feel the slight tremble of her body, and as they moved politely, formally, to the music, the contact was simply not enough. 'Let's get out of here.'

She nodded and before the last dance had even faded Rafiq was leading her outside, only not through the main entrance. 'We cannot be seen…' he told her.

'I don't understand.'

'There are a lot of press outside.'

He seemed different, more austere. He'd held her back when they danced. Even now he seemed to be hurrying her when surely he should be taking her in his arms or at the very least holding her hand.

There was a car waiting and a driver too, as well as a couple of men who were walking both behind and in front of them, and then she saw the diplomatic plates on the car.

And she'd been too scared perhaps to hear before, but right now she simply had to know who he was.

'Rafiq, who are you?'

'We will speak when we are alone,' Rafiq responded. 'I thought we could go to my residence, or back to Haven Manor.'

'No, tell me now.' She halted him. Ready now to know. 'Tell me,' she insisted. 'Who are you?'

He gestured to the men around him to step well back. 'We can talk in the car, not out on the street.'

'Tell me who you are, Rafiq, before I get in the car.'

'Very well,' he nodded. 'I am royal. I know it can sound a little daunting—'

'How royal?' She cut him off with a question, thought back to the deference with which he'd been treated at Haven Manor, as if nothing had been too much trouble from the second he'd arrived. And now this security detail, the car, the everything. 'How royal are we talking, Rafiq?'

'I am…' Oh, she looked up at him, and somehow knew he was more than a minor royal, more than some vague prince and then he confirmed it. 'I am the crown prince of Al-Zahir.'

'Crown prince.' Liliana frowned. 'Does that mean…?' Her throat felt too tight and there was this need almost to put her hand down low on her stomach, but she fought it. Did not want to give him a hint to the chance of a life that for the past few weeks she'd been trying to deny. But if Rafiq was a crown prince, did that mean…? 'You're the heir?' she queried.

'Correct.'

And it was too much.

Just by far too much.

And no, Liliana's reaction was not one he was used to, for she shook her head. 'I need to go.'

'Liliana…' He caught her arm as she turned to flee.

'Rafiq, I don't know what to say.'

'Say nothing, at least until you have heard what I came here to say.'

'No.' She shook her head, thinking of how they had slipped out of a side exit and rather guessed theirs was not a relationship that would be considered suitable.

God alone knew what it meant if she was pregnant.

'I don't want to hear it.' She took a shaky breath. 'I need to go.'

'Not yet.' He stepped forward, his hand still upon her upper arm, but she wrenched it away.

'You said that the moment I felt uncomfortable I could leave.'

'I did,' he conceded, dropping contact.

'Then I'm leaving.'

'At least allow my driver to take you wherever you need to go.'

'I don't need your driver, Rafiq.'

She spun on her heels and with a sob ran off, back into the throng of photographers and models leaving, and the line of limousines, waiting to collect, but she ran in the opposite direction and was grateful to see the line-up of taxis.

She was scared.

Scared that she was pregnant.

Scared of the desire that still coursed after months apart. More, she was scared that this could be her life. Tumbling into bed when the crown prince graced London. She thought how he'd told her about his lovers…

She thought of that moment of possession, and his words, *Rafiq would not like it*, and even then, even with her lack of experience she'd known that he meant it. Of course he would expect she remain exclusive to him…

From one night in his bed, she already knew that.

He had made her his lover and made her his.

'Where to?' the taxi driver asked, and she thought of the gifts he'd sent. How, thanks to the lift he'd arranged, he knew where she lived. So, instead of asking to be taken to her home, she gave the address of her mother.

Oh, she touched her arm where his fingers had just been and could still feel the warmth and bliss of his touch,

No, she wasn't scared of Rafiq.

What scared her was that she might say yes.

Liliana's phone was flat by morning.

The battery drained by her frantic searches.

Al-Zahir, famed for pearl diving…check. And yes, he'd been schooled here in England—everything he had told her was true, except… There was so much that he had left out.

Rafiq had been born third in line to the throne. And while Rafiq had told her that his brother had died, he hadn't told her the details. Or about the dreadful conflict that had long ago raged between the neighbouring countries but had flared up again fifteen or so years ago.

Rafiq's father, the King of Al-Zahir, had endorsed the coup and had refused to retract his support when Khalid had been taken prisoner while riding in the Al-Zahir desert.

A few days later Rafiq had been ambushed in London

and taken to Al-Nawar, where he'd too been held for the best part of a year.

The details were sketchy as to his capture and the conditions in which he'd been held, but Liliana closed her eyes in horror when she found out it was there that Khalid had died.

Had they been held together? she wondered.

And what had Rafiq meant when he'd said that Khalid had betrayed him?

She thought of the brutal scarring that laced his beautiful body.

'Don't ask,' he had warned on the night they had met.

And now she bumbled through translations and found out he had somehow escaped from his captors. The miraculous feat unleashed the momentum that had finally toppled the despot king.

Then she read a few articles and reports about him and there were times she wondered if they were discussing the same man, if she'd somehow got things wrong, because the Rafiq they discussed was described as solemn, harsh…

Cold.

There was nothing about lovers that she could see, no relationships of note, but just as she'd exhaled in relief she clicked on another article and read that it was believed he kept a harem.

'Oh, my God…'

It had almost been a relief when her phone battery died.

'Lili…' There was a knock on the bedroom door and her mother brought her in a mug of tea. 'Is everything okay?'

'Everything's fine,' she attempted to deflect, but of course, arriving unannounced in a ball gown last night was going to require a little more explanation than the vague excuse she'd offered last night. Still she doubled down on it, muttering something about rideshare. 'It was just easier to come here.'

'Lili?'

Liliana could hear the dubious note and question in her mother's tone. 'I was just…' She *really* didn't like to talk about her personal life, even within her personal life! 'I'm avoiding someone,' she admitted.

'That awful manager?'

Liliana gave a noncommittal smile; it felt easier to let her mother think she was avoiding Simon than telling her about Rafiq…

'You can talk to me, Liliana.'

'I know that I can.' Liliana nodded and thought of Rafiq, how he'd simply stated he didn't want to reveal things, and the honesty they had both found that night somehow strengthened her. 'I'm just not ready to.'

'Fair enough.'

With that out of the way it was actually nice being at her mother's and when she suggested she stay another night, Liliana agreed.

Her mother's phone charger didn't fit her phone, and that rather helped matters! She was scared what more she'd find out.

And while she didn't think Rafiq would be pounding on her door or anything…she wasn't hiding from him.

Maybe a bit.

It was just nice to be home and in her childhood bed

and to spend some quiet time with her mother. And for the first time in years, she asked after her father.

'Do you ever see him?'

'No…' Her mother thought for a moment. 'We spoke a few months ago, but he hasn't been down to visit lately.'

'Why would you still let him visit you?'

'Lili, please…' Her mother closed her tired eyes. 'I don't expect you to understand.'

Rafiq, though unused to women fleeing in terror when they found out about his title, knew she was simply overwhelmed.

Late on the Sunday night he had decided he would send flowers, perhaps to her work, at least give her his number, because if she felt even a tenth of what he was feeling, then Liliana must ache with need….

'Sir.'

He frowned as Salar knocked at the door to the drawing room.

'I have a call for you.'

Rafiq nodded, hoping it was somehow Liliana while knowing that was impossible, since few could access his private line.

Of course it wasn't her and he rolled his eyes at the sound of Yara's voice.

'You could have at least warned me,' she said.

'About what?'

'I was giving a speech when the news first broke.'

'What news?'

It didn't take long to find what Yara was talking about. There were photos of him and Liliana, not just of last night, but there were photos of them kissing by the lake, even a picture of them staring into each other's eyes on the underground.

'Tomorrow's papers are going to be full of it,' Yara sighed. 'Both here and there.'

'Yara, I had no idea…'

'I know you didn't,' she sighed. 'I should thank you really—I have every reason not to marry you now. The thing is, Rafiq, I know you didn't do this for me.'

'I didn't.'

Yara knew him well enough to know that his no had meant no.

'And that scares me, Rafiq.'

'Scares you?'

'These photos have been taken months apart. The way you hold her tells me it's serious.'

Rafiq was silent.

'So,' Yara asked. 'What have you told her?'

'Yara, stop.' He could not think of Yara now and her damn secret. His only thought was Liliana waking to this disaster and the hell that was about to enter her world.

Oh, he knew how bad this would be.

But Yara made it all about her. 'I have long dreaded you falling in love.' She started to cry. 'It isn't just torture that drags out our secrets, Rafiq.'

'What are you talking about?'

'Love makes you bare your soul.'

'Yara, how many times do I have to tell you I'm not going to…' He paused then, for it dawned that he couldn't tell even Liliana the truth—that he wasn't the cheating bastard the media now claimed him to be. 'Could you…?' He stopped himself from asking Yara to share with Liliana her secret.

'Maybe we should just get married, Rafiq. I think it would be easier. While my father was initially furious with you, my mother seems to think this has all happened because we waited too long.'

'Let's just see what happens,' he said far more calmly than he felt.

'I'm scared. Please, promise me that you haven't told her.'

'Yara,' he said, his voice flat, 'I gave you my word.'

And his word meant an awful lot.

'Balach, I can help,' Rafiq insisted. 'With your daughter's surgery.'

'Oh, so you're a doctor?' he sneered.

'I am crown prince.'

It was the first time he had said it out loud and in doing so it acknowledged Khalid's death and twisted the knife that felt lodged in his heart. Yet, there was an authority to those words, his new title held weight, and even if they were sworn enemies Rafiq saw Balach's spine straighten.

'I would see she got the surgery she requires. The best hospital, the best doctors...'

Balach was silent.

'I don't ask you to trust me,' Rafiq said. 'I ask you to come to Al-Zahir with me. You and your wife and the baby. I am too weak to make it alone.'

'It's too dangerous,' Balach said.

But Rafiq could see him waver.

By Monday, Liliana was walking from the tube to work in a rather tight pencil skirt she had found in her old wardrobe—though she'd probably been eighteen the last time she'd worn it. Her mother had given her a pale blue silk top to wear and in the cupboard under the stairs she'd found a pair of wedges.

Gosh, it wasn't really the best look for such a high-end fashion house but for today it would just have to do.

Only it wasn't the rather cobbled-together look that was troubling Liliana as she made her way out of the underground. It wasn't even the thought of facing her colleagues, and their inevitable questions about her incredibly dashing date…

It wasn't even Rafiq…

Rather, it wasn't *entirely* Rafiq that consumed her mind this morning, but a thought that for weeks she'd been trying to ignore. She'd kept telling herself that things would be fine. They'd used protection after all…

Except.

Seeing Rafiq and finding out about his might and power had told her she could bury her head no more.

Pausing outside an out-of-hours chemist, she caught sight of her reflection in a mirrored panel and knew she had to find out one way or the other.

And then work out what to do.

Stepping in, she made her purchase and slipped the test into her vast bag.

She'd do the test tonight, Liliana told herself as she made her way to work…

There were photographers gathering outside the offices, and she guessed they had someone famous inside. Honestly, some celebrities squeezed in these appointments at the oddest hours, but then all thought stopped. A hand gripped her upper arm and a body blocked her and she had the feeling of being enveloped by another. And just when surely she should have been drenched in terror, instead, without turning her head, before she could offer a startled shout, she knew that it was Rafiq. She recognised his scent; her skin knew his touch.

'What on earth…?' And then fear arrived as she realised Rafiq was pulling her towards a car, the door being held open by one of the suited men she'd seen on leaving the ball. 'Get off me…'

'Be quiet,' he warned, 'don't make a scene, they haven't spotted you yet.'

'Who?'

'The press.'

And it dawned she was not being kidnapped; she was being bundled into a vehicle for her own protection—the reporters were there waiting for her! In the back of his vehicle, behind darkened windows, she found out why.

'Our affair has been exposed.'

'Affair?' She gave an incredulous laugh and shook her head. 'Hardly!'

'Liliana, you need to listen carefully.' His voice was grave and she saw then the dark rings under his eyes and the grim expression on his face. 'There are photos of us all over the place. My people are trying to get them taken down as we speak. I assure you this will be sorted.'

'What photos…?' She gave a bemused shake of her head. 'We danced once…' And barely at that, she thought, recalling how he'd held her at a distance, like some duty dance with an aunt at a wedding. 'We didn't so much as kiss…' But then her voice faded as she looked down at his phone and she saw a photo of them in much earlier days, sitting on the tube, and both smiling into each other's eyes.

Her own eyes widened, and she looked urgently to him. 'We're not doing anything…' But as he swiped the images her voice turned off, as if a remote control had been touched and the sound snapped off. There by a dark lake they embraced…their first kiss recorded, their beautiful private first contact now shared for all to see.

'So what?' She leapt to their defence. 'We're not hurting anyone, we're both single.'

'Correct,' he said, and then she closed her eyes as the 'but' came. 'But in the eyes of my people and the people of Al-Nawar…' He hesitated, and it was the first time she had seen him falter.

'Let me see the headlines.'

'First let me explain.'

'No,' she retorted, and when he didn't hand over his phone, she found a charger, and plugged in her own.

'Liliana, if you hadn't run off the other night, I would have told you all of this,' he said as her phone came to life and she sat skimming the articles, swiping through photos.

'It says here that your fiancée was in London that day. That she visited you at your home.'

'Yara is not, nor has she ever been, my fiancée.'

'I think your people might dispute that fact. It says here that you're promised to each other.'

'It has never been official. That is a promise our parents made.'

She breathed in sharply as another woman's face came on the screen. She had long black hair and stunning almond-shaped black eyes, and was as polished and elegant as the cheat that sat beside Liliana now.

She felt ill as she read the headline: 'Princess Yara's Heart Shattered.'

'How could you?' She shook her head and handed him back his phone. There was nothing more she needed to see, not with Rafiq present anyway. 'Do you know what? I don't even want to hear your excuses. Can you ask your driver to drop me home?'

'You can't go home yet. I can guarantee that the press is going to be there.'

'If he isn't going to take me home then I'll get out now and make my own way.'

'Liliana, you need to hear what I have to say.' He glanced in the direction of his driver. 'We'll talk properly when we're alone.'

'I never want to be alone again with you,' she retorted. 'I mean it, Rafiq, just take me home.'

Reluctantly he gave his driver orders and given it was peak-hour traffic, the journey was impossibly slow as Rafiq's excuses came thick and fast.

'You and I were seen together on two separate nights and that is what has caused the problem.'

She stared ahead.

'There are strict edicts...'

'Are you promised to Yara? Betrothed, engaged, dating?' She glared at him then. 'I didn't realise I had to give you a selection, or be so specific. I thought I made it clear I would not see you if you were involved with anyone.' Her voice rose. 'Or promised to anyone...'

The car was turning into her street, the location Liliana had insisted she be taken to, but panic struck, for photographers were already there. And when she demanded that the car turn around and take her to her mother's it was precisely then that her mother rang.

'Mum.' Liliana did all she could to keep her voice calm even as her mother informed her that there were photographers outside her home too. 'Just pull the curtains and ignore them,' Liliana said. 'And don't answer the door.'

'Is this why you hid here this weekend?'

'I wasn't hiding,' Liliana said, but her voice cracked then and when tears started to fall, Rafiq took the phone.

Oh, the perfect prince he was at his silken smooth best. He first apologised for the stress this was causing then told her mother how his people were taking care of things now and that very soon the photographers would be gone. Reassuring her that there had been a slight miscommunication. His voice was so measured it was almost soothing—of course this would soon be sorted out, but it might take a little time for it all to calm down.

Then, having calmed her mother down, Liliana listened as he told her his plans.

'Ms Hamilton, we're going to get you to a hotel until it's all died down. There's a car coming for you now,' Rafiq said and to Liliana that sounded like the best idea, but then she frantically shook her head as he spoke on. 'Liliana has agreed to come to Al-Zahir until I've sorted out the press and had all the articles and photos taken down, and she'll return when it's yesterday's news.'

'No,' Liliana mouthed, shaking her head. 'No way,' she insisted when he'd ended the call. 'I'll go to the hotel with my mother.'

'And you'll be outed. Your picture is all over the place,

you'll be recognised in a matter of moments. I'm sure now that there was a spotter on the train. Usually I notice them...' He was honest. 'In fact, I did, but then you boarded and I forgot about him.'

'I saw him.' She thought back to the man in the grey cap and how he'd been looking over to Rafiq.

She thought of the pack of reporters waiting at her work, then at her mother's. And then flicked through the photos, again hating that their first kiss was out for public consumption.

It felt as if the whole of London was chasing her.

It felt like it had when her father's wife had found out.

Panic started to hit, the enormity of it all, her pulse was roaring in her ears and she massaged her temples. She could feel the colour leaching from her face and though sitting down felt close to a faint, she leaned forward. 'I can't deal with this, Rafiq.'

'Then let me.'

His voice was low and calm, but even more soothing was the light touch of his hand on her back, a touch so light yet it felt as if he took the weight of the world from her a little.

'I don't have my passport.'

'Tell me where it is and give me your keys. Salar will sort it.'

She was angry and confused—more than she could express, but with that touch somehow he conveyed that he would get her through this.

That she could let go of the fear.

'My plane is waiting. You'll be away from all this before you know it and I'll join you as soon as I can.'

'You're not coming with me?'

'First I need to sort things out for your mother, for you…' He hesitated for a second and perhaps chose to be honest. 'We can't be seen together, even at the airport.'

'Because of Yara?'

Rafiq closed his eyes in frustration. Salar was driving, the privacy screen closed and while he wanted to trust him, while Salar was helping get Liliana to safety, still he did not feel he could freely speak.

'We'll talk when I get there. For now, you will be taken care of in my desert abode…'

'Hidden away.' Her spine stiffened and he removed his touch as if registering she neither wanted it nor needed it now. Her voice was flat when it came. 'I'll be taken care of as your lover…' She glared at him. 'Was that what you were going to ask me on Saturday night?'

'Let us talk in the desert.' He breathed deeply in. 'I know that this must all have come as a shock.'

'A slight understatement.'

'You also know that we do need to work things out.'

She stayed silent.

They did have to speak, Liliana knew that…but whatever was shared she would not be revealing her fears that she might be pregnant. She would work *them* out first, though she could not envisage how.

'And if I want to leave…' Her voice trailed off.

'My promise remains. You can leave anytime.'

That side of Rafiq she trusted.

It was the only reason she agreed to fly to Al-Zahir.

CHAPTER EIGHT

LILIANA WAS TAKEN to a private terminal and shown to an elegant lounge, where she waited for Salar to return with her passport.

'Excellent,' the assistant said once it had been produced. 'We'll just sort out the paperwork and then we'll get you airside.'

'Airside?'

'Through customs.'

'I see.'

She didn't really.

Salar headed back to Rafiq's side, and Liliana was handed over to various staff.

The day was a blur of private lounges and being discreetly dealt with both in London and Al-Zahir.

Flying across vast swathes of desert, she had never felt more scared and alone. And so angry, not just with Rafiq, but with herself for sleeping with a man who clearly wasn't free.

Her first time in a helicopter was alone, and the reddening sky painted the sands pink and then, when they must be deep in the desert, she first glimpsed the compound. There were several domed tents surrounding a larger central one, and as the chopper drew closer, she saw that a couple seemed linked to the main one. Liliana could even see horses circling in a large yard, perhaps unnerved by the lights and noise of the chopper, and she looked to the central tent that for now she would call…

Not home.

'Here.'

An escort gave her a scarf to wear before they came in to land and Liliana soon found out why. It was like opening an oven door as she stepped down from the helicopter. The rotors were blowing up hot sand that stung her bare legs and she was grateful for the scarf shielding her mouth and eyes.

The assistant took her to the entrance and then gave her a nod.

'Wait…' Liliana called. She wanted to know how long she would be here for, or when Rafiq would arrive, but the assistant was already making a dash back to the helicopter. But then the entrance to the abode was opened and Liliana was met with a smiling face.

'Liliana.' A woman introduced herself as Fatima, and hung up her scarf and pointed to some jewelled slippers for her to change into. 'You have had such a long journey. Let me show you around…' She frowned and peered behind where Liliana stood. 'You have no luggage?'

'None,' Liliana said, clutching her shoulder bag, the only things she'd brought with her. 'I didn't exactly have time to pack.'

Of course Fatima didn't understand, nor need her slight sarcasm.

'I haven't got anything with me,' Liliana corrected. 'It was a bit of a rush.'

‘That’s fine,’ Fatima said and smiled. ‘We have everything you need here. First I will show you around.’

She was led along a corridor of white and brought to the very centre.

‘The main abode,’ Fatima said. It was indeed at the centre, and incredibly quiet. There was a central fire pit with a long flue that led to the ceiling, though the fire wasn’t lit. Around it were cushions and low tables.

‘It will be cool soon,’ Fatima said. ‘I shall light it before I leave.’

‘Leave?’

‘I have quarters nearby. You pull one of the ropes in your sleeping area if you need me. The rest are for the crown prince.’

‘I see.’

‘Crown Prince Rafiq usually calls for breakfast at seven, and he tends to take dinner quite late. We only come when summoned…’

‘We?’ Liliana questioned.

‘There are several staff, mostly for the crown prince, but I am assigned to care for you. If you have any questions, please don’t trouble the other staff with them. I take care of private matters.’

The desert abode was stunning. The floors were covered in gorgeous Persian rugs, and there were also tapestries, softening the dark of the furniture, but nothing could soften her thoughts.

Did Fatima consider her one of the crown prince’s private matters?

Clearly.

Liliana wondered, she truly did, what he had been going to suggest had she not fled after the ball…

She had thought he might ask her to be his London lover.

Now she was wondering if he'd been going to ask her to join his harem.

She felt ill at the thought.

She was shown behind intricate lattice screens to a dining area, and Fatima invited her to take some refreshments before they continued the tour.

'You have travelled a long way—you look tired.'

There was a plate of fruits which Liliana didn't want—and little silver bowls piled high with Turkish delight, which Liliana didn't like and so she declined them, but feeling rude she accepted a drink of cool mint tea.

It was delicious.

Cold, minty and honey sweet, it steadied her enough to be shown to the sleeping area.

It was separate from the living area and darker. Fatima lit oil lamps as she led the way.

There were several small rooms with pretty muslin drapes tied back and they looked like beauty areas; she glimpsed a massage table, a beauty room… Instantly she knew when she came to his, for it was by far the largest and the bed was draped with furs.

There was another fire pit, again unlit.

'The seraglio is through there…' Fatima pointed to soft veils that lined one of the tent walls.

'Seraglio?'

'A private chamber for women.'

'Is there another entrance?'

'Of course.' Fatima smiled. 'You don't disturb him unless summoned.'

He'd damn well better not.

'Thank you,' she said through taut lips, and they further tightened as they stepped in the seraglio. In the centre was a bed, dressed in violet silks, but Liliana's eyes kept flicking to the veils that would separate her from his chamber.

Fatima pulled back the drapes on a stunning wardrobe. There were robes of velvet in every colour, beautiful flowing fabrics, and though Liliana wore only the clothes she'd put on this morning, she vowed there and then she would not be wearing something another of his lovers had worn.

'Through here…' Fatima guided. 'This is the Diwan Al-Zayn—it means Chamber of Adornment.'

Liliana felt her throat constrict, but even if somewhat appalled, she was also fascinated.

It was really rather beautiful, a private, elegant space with mirrors and also what looked like a massage table, and beside it, *hammam* towels. There was a deep bath that would be drawn for her each evening, Fatima explained.

No doubt, in preparedness for him.

'I shall serve dinner…' Fatima started, but again Liliana shook her head.

'I'm fine, I ate on the plane.' Her stomach was heaving just looking at the perfumes and jewels she could select from.

'Then I shall prepare the Diwan Al-Zayn for you…'

No, Liliana was about to say, but then halted. She was not preparing herself for him, but certainly she needed to wash. As well as that her body ached from too many shots of adrenaline, not just from her journey, but from seeing him again…

And yes, she was curious too.

She was given a silk bathing robe, which she accepted and put on, and while the bath was being prepared Liliana stripped off her too tight skirt and rinsed out her bra and knickers in the sink area in her room.

'Liliana…'

Fatima called her in, and the bath was steamy and the air fragrant with rosewater. There were even petals floating on top of the water.

'Thank you,' Liliana said, expecting Fatima to leave, but she didn't.

'Please.' She gestured to the bath. 'I will start with your hair.'

Oh, she wasn't to float in the dreamy bath, and let the tension go on her day; there was actually quite a lot to be done before Fatima considered her ready for the prince.

It made her angry, but she wanted the knowledge, wanted to know his lovers' rituals, and just to know…

First her hair was saturated in a creamy concoction, then wrapped. All too soon she lay on the massage table, salt being rubbed into her skin, and every inch of her tidied…a little like the *everything* shower she had done in preparation for the ball, only with a lot more components.

Her eyebrows were threaded, her legs, her bikini line too.

And then, with her skin pink and shiny, she sat on a stool as Fatima picked up a large copper jug and the hair mask was rinsed off.

The more polished she got, the angrier she became, because it made the wonderful spontaneous night they had shared impossibly out of reach.

'There.' Fatima combed her hair, and then wrapped

it gently in a towel. 'It will be very silky. I make the cream myself.'

'Do you?'

Liliana liked Fatima, who chatted quietly away, never startling her, but she was also incredibly direct and practical. 'Now I oil your skin.'

'I can do that.'

'Not correctly.'

She should be too upset to relax, but it really was rather blissful, her cares somewhat melted away by Fatima's skilled hands, and then she was given a sheer muslin nightdress which Fatima told her she had made just this afternoon.

Wrapped in towels, Liliana admired Fatima's handiwork. It was white, with silk on the hems and delicately hand stitched. 'It's very beautiful.'

'Thank you. Now I suggest that you try and get some sleep,' Fatima told her. 'The oils will make you tired… Please call if you need anything.'

And she was left alone.

The next thing she did was go through her bag to get her phone, but first her fingers closed on a paper bag. Taking it out, she realised it was the pregnancy test she had bought just this morning.

Possibly the sensible course of action would be to take the test now. To know what she was dealing with before Rafiq arrived…

But then she thought of that morning, lying in his arms, and Rafiq asking what she would do with her day…

I can't hide from you.

She couldn't.

Her feelings, her fears, her emotions all seemed to

bubble to the surface when he was close, and she did not know how to meet those silvery eyes and lie…

It was better not to know.

And so, she buried the test at the very bottom of her vast bag and then took out her phone.

Of course there was no signal.

Liliana dressed. The nightgown was long, down past her knees, but its sheerness didn't allow it to be called modest and it clung a little to her oiled body. Still, it was a relief to be out of that tight skirt and bra, and to have bare feet after a day in ill-fitting wedges.

Her bed was like a cloud, and she lay there, listening to the sounds of wind.

Certain she would never sleep…

Rafiq arrived deep into the night wondering if he should have chosen firefighter as a profession, for he was certainly putting many out now. He had finally sorted the damn press when Yara had called, repeating that it might be better if he were to announce they would marry. Again he had told her to wait, and just when he had thought he could get to Liliana he had landed in Al-Zahir to be told the king wished to speak with him.

'I will bring him up to speed soon,' Rafiq had said, striding towards the chopper.

'Your Highness, it is an official summons from the king.'

Rafiq's back had stiffened; his father had never done that before.

He did not want to go into the palace; he wanted to get back to Liliana, but of course there could be no ignoring a direct summons.

Shortly after landing, he found himself on his way to the sanctum at the very centre of the Al-Zahir palace.

It was magnificent. There were no windows on the high stone walls, just a huge clear dome above that let in light relative to the time of day.

It afforded the same light as the desert, the same light as the sea, the same light for the wisest of men or the most foolish…

Rafiq strode through the softly lit palace, still wearing a suit and tie, angry at being summoned, preferring to discuss this with Liliana before his father, but as he stood at the guarded entrance and waited to be let in it dawned on him again…

He could never fully discuss this with Liliana.

Never tell her the real reason he resisted marriage.

He stepped into the relative darkness of the sanctum, lit only by a sliver of new moon, but the architects of ancient times had been wise and the upper walls were lined with pearls from Al-Zahir's plentiful ocean and they enhanced the thin light.

He made his way over to where the king stood in the centre.

'You should know better, Rafiq.'

Rafiq offered no response.

'I have given you great leeway. I have not forced you into marriage. You can do what you want behind closed doors and veils, but here you are seen being affectionate with the same woman three months apart. Dancing, kissing… You know the edicts forbid this.'

'They don't,' Rafiq said through gritted teeth, 'because Yara and I are not betrothed.'

'There is a silent agreement,' his father barked. 'And

both countries know it! You have brought shame to both peoples.'

'Where?' Rafiq said. 'Our people seem fine. There is no baying mob outside the palace. If anything, they seem surprised to learn that I am capable of affection.'

'Well, you have brought shame to Princess Yara. King Al-Nawar and I are both in full agreement—you are to apologise on national television.'

'Never.'

'I shall remind you to whom you are speaking. You *shall* apologise on national television and speak of your desire for unity between the two countries. Shortly thereafter you shall visit King Al-Nawar in his inner sanctum, then you *shall* call for Yara to be your bride.'

'You cannot force me.'

'Incorrect,' the king said. 'You must be aware than I am permitted to call for your bride.'

'Don't even try it,' Rafiq warned. 'Surely the groom being dragged to the ceremony chained and bound would cause even greater offence. And don't think I wouldn't do it.' He held up his wrists, displaying the scars. 'Being chained and bound is nothing new to me!'

'Rafiq, there was an agreement. Not officially perhaps, but there has long been an understanding that you and Yara shall marry. You cannot deny that. You went along with it, Rafiq.'

And only Rafiq and Yara knew why.

Instead of revealing that though, he countered with an attack. 'For nine months the two of you left me there to rot. Even after they had killed Khalid you did nothing to get me out.' His voice husked, and he saw the pain flash in his father's eyes at the mention of his brother, and he steadied his tone. 'I shall choose when I marry. If I marry…'

'You need an heir, Rafiq,' his father said. 'A suitable heir, and for that you need a suitable wife.'

'I am going to the desert.'

He strode off, but before he could knock on the door for the guards to open up, his father called out to him.

'Rafiq.'

He turned.

'I did what I could to get you free.'

'Well, it wasn't enough.'

'I just wish you…' He stopped talking, shook his head.

'You wish it had been me that died?'

'Of course not.'

'And Khalid had been the one to live?'

'That is not what I was about to say.'

'What then?' Rafiq challenged, but his father gave a shake of his head. Conversation closed.

Rafiq went to knock on the door to be let out rather than respond, but before they opened his father spoke.

'Perhaps run through the edicts regarding discretion with your mistress.'

He turned. 'Do not call her that.'

'Rafiq.' His father even sounded sympathetic. 'That is all she can ever be.'

Flying to his desert abode, he could feel the pressure from all sides.

Even Yara seemed to be caving in and wanting this marriage.

Then he thought of what his father had said, or rather had stopped himself from saying.

Of course he must deep down wish it had been Khalid who had lived. He'd have been married for a long time by now, and the children he and his wife would undoubtedly have had by now would be teenagers.

Rafiq closed his eyes, wondering how it was possible to miss nieces and nephews that he had never had, but yes, it felt as if a part of his soul had left him that day, and yet he was so cross with his brother too.

Glancing down at the abode from the sky, he felt tense shoulders drop a fraction, felt the pall of grief lift. Realised he was smiling, simply that she was here…

Even if there were difficult conversations to be had.

Even if there were conversations that could never be had.

His world was made better from knowing Liliana was near.

Only there was no angry Liliana to greet him when he entered the abode, no trace of her summery scent in the air. Nor was she waiting, as he'd both secretly hoped though very much doubted, in his bed. Instead, he found her asleep in the seraglio.

'Liliana?'

She did not stir.

'Liliana?' He was not used to having to wake anyone. Certainly he had hoped they could at least talk. He turned on the lamp and was about to touch her shoulder to rouse her when he saw she was deeply asleep. Her hair was splayed on the violet cushion, the tense features he had left her with now softened in sleep. And he felt those damn feelings again, and could not bear to disturb her. 'Get some rest,' he said, and was about to turn off the lamp off when her eyes opened.

'Hey,' he said.

Liliana had slept through the fire being lit in his sleeping area, and the woodsy scent had seemed to come from the fire that had danced on the night they'd made love. She'd somehow managed to incorporate the sound of the helicopter approaching into her dream.

An odd dream where she and Rafiq were flying over London, on their way to Haven Manor.

She'd opened her eyes to his impossibly good looks and for a second all had been right in the world.

He was wearing a suit and looked…

She'd frowned then, because he looked, well, not dreadful, but he looked tousled, and the dark rings under his eyes spoke of his strain.

'Rafiq!'

He was here.

Her instinct was to kneel up. To jump up in the bed and walk on her knees to him, to just wrap herself around him and be enveloped in his arms. His eyes had an opaque desirous sheen, as if all he wanted was the same.

But by then she'd stopped dreaming and recalling all that had occurred and right now, she didn't trust him, nor her instincts.

'Go away!' she told him.

'Liliana.' He did not have the patience for this. 'Clearly we need to talk.'

'Perhaps,' she responded, not liking the rather brusque, impatient man who stood by her bed, though wanting him all the same. 'But it will be at a time of my choosing.'

She rolled onto her side, turned her back to him, because it was either that or leap into his arms.

Rafiq could not believe she would dismiss him like that, that she would simply turn her back on him.

'Liliana,' he demanded.

'I don't jump to your command, Rafiq.' She rolled onto her back and looked up at him. 'And don't you dare try to summon me.' She gestured to the veils. 'Is that what you do?' She was appalled, her angry eyes demanding contrition from him. 'Just pull a rope when you want sex?'

'Sometimes.' He nodded, a slight smile on his face and no trace of contrition in those silvery eyes. 'But don't worry—' that smile was just a little cruel '—I shan't be calling you. I like my lovers a little less surly.'

'Bastard!'

'No,' he said, 'I am not. I am doing everything I can to do the right thing by you.'

He turned on his heel and walked out.

She breathed out when he left the seraglio and then breathed in the traces of his scent. And the tent wasn't private. There were the shadows of the fires in both the sleeping and the lounge areas dancing on the walls of her room. And when he stood, she could see him, even when she lay on her back, because there were times his shadow stretched across the ceiling.

And she could hear him.

While being served his meal, soft music played, and then she lay with her back to his chamber, listening to him undress, and every fibre of her being was fighting itself not to step through that veil.

Of course they needed to talk.

But somehow, she understood her mother now…

Rafiq made her weak.

CHAPTER NINE

LILIANA AWOKE LATE.

Extremely late.

For a moment she lay there wondering how she could possibly have slept in when there was much to sort out. Or how she could relax in such an unfamiliar place.

She washed her face and hands then brushed her teeth and then pulled on the bra and knickers she'd washed out last night.

Her pencil skirt seemed even tighter than yesterday, but hopefully she was just bloated and about to get her period. Still, just in case she had the beginnings of a bump, she left her blouse untucked. Pulling on the jewelled slippers, she checked her reflection and was rather relieved to look dreadful.

Liliana was not here to impress Rafiq, nor succumb to his charms.

She was here to find out what had occurred and how he intended to fix things.

And then get out.

Then her eyes drifted down to her stomach…

There was no way she would be telling him her suspicions about the pregnancy.

Not here.

She put her hand over her stomach as she'd wanted to the other night, as if protecting the little life within.

'Not here,' she promised. 'I shan't be telling him here.'

Stepping out of the seraglio, she was very grateful he had shared the photos of his horse with her that first day. Otherwise the sight of Rafiq dressed in black desert robes might have had her turn and flee. Even with the small heads-up, the imposing sight of him had her step falter.

He was seated on a cushion, reading through some papers, and at the sound of her coming out looked up, his eyes narrowing.

He was a formidable sight indeed.

'Good God,' he said, those silver eyes taking in her attire, and coming to rest in her gaze. 'What on earth are you wearing?'

'The same clothes I had on yesterday.'

'But surely there are robes, I told Fatima to ensure a full selection.'

'I'm not dressing from your harem's wardrobe.'

'Harem?'

'I've read about you and it's rumoured you keep one.'

'Of course it is.' He shrugged. 'I don't.'

'Well, I'm not dressing from your lovers' wardrobe.'

'Up to you.' He stood and gestured for her to join him in the dining area behind the screens. 'Shall we have some breakfast?' Then he added, 'Or would that be brunch?'

She smiled to herself as she lowered herself to a cushion at the low table, for she heard the inference. 'Did you expect me to be up and ready to attend to your needs?'

'I never really know what to expect from you,' Rafiq

said. 'I thought you would be waiting last night with many questions. I have to say I'm impressed.'

'Well, I'm not,' Liliana said, taking some soft bread and scooping up some delicacies. 'In fact, I'm very unimpressed of late.' She lifted her eyes to him accusingly. 'I actually preferred not knowing who you were.'

'You prefer to bury your head in the sand?'

'We should have left things as they were. I wish I'd never found out about Yara.'

'Take out the drama of Yara,' Rafiq said. 'Are you saying that you wish I hadn't come to your ball?'

'Yes,' she said, and then thought of all those awful nights full of longing, all those tears she had cried wishing she could see him again and the sheer unadulterated thrill when she had. The way her heart had leapt at the sound of him calling her name. She shrugged tightly. 'I don't know,' Liliana admitted. 'But it's rather hard to take out the drama of Yara. I asked you outright if you were married and you specifically told me that you didn't date…'

'And I answered truthfully—I am not married, and I don't date, and Yara and I are not betrothed, well, not officially. Our parents came to an agreement long ago. They decided between themselves that when the time came it would unite the countries, but it was never announced, and the truth of the matter is that neither of us really want the marriage.'

'My father used to do this to my mother, make excuses, offer explanations—'

'I am not your father,' he abruptly cut in. 'Let's make that perfectly clear. I am a man of my word and I am explaining things as best I can.' Without revealing a secret he had not just promised to keep, but was not even his to share. 'Yara and I have little to do with each other, except…'

'Except you were in London together on the day we met,' Liliana said. 'I've read all the details now. I know she was at your house on the day we met. So you don't have "little to do with each other".'

'You will listen to me…'

She looked up from the mint tea she was drinking, and heard the edge to his tone, and knew he was not used to being spoken back to. 'No, you will listen to me,' Liliana said, 'and you will answer my questions.' But even with brave words her eyes were sparkling with tears. 'Firstly, is my mother safe?'

'Safe?'

'Yes, safe?'

'Of course she is…' he snapped back, but then conceded that with the press hounding her, Liliana's mother might have felt otherwise. 'Yes, she is at a hotel.'

'I don't want her name being dragged through the mud.' Her voice sounded strangled. 'She's been through enough.'

'I know she has. The reporters are gone from your homes and the articles are being wiped from the Internet.'

'How?'

'My office has taken care of most of it, but it wasn't that easy. I've had to agree to a live interview…' He hissed out a breath. 'On top of that, both kings want me to publicly apologise.'

'Perhaps you should apologise,' Liliana said, 'to *all* parties concerned.'

His jaw clamped down, and he looked at Liliana—so wary, confused and angry.

'I assure you that your mother is fine. She could go home today, but she said that she would rather stay for a few more days at the Ritz Carlton,' he said, then added, a little sardonically, 'just to be sure.'

He watched her lips twitch a little as she fought not to smile, perhaps imaging her mother enjoying her luxurious surrounds. 'That makes you smile.'

'Yes,' she admitted. 'She works very hard. I'm sure she's enjoying being spoilt for a couple of days.'

He watched as she nibbled at a pastry, but then seemed to give in and put it down on the copper plate, as if even the effort of eating was too much. 'You look tired,' Rafiq said, not liking how the sunny woman he had met now looked pale and worried, or rather, not liking that he had made her so. 'Upset.'

'Of course I am—you've turned me into my mother and I shall never forgive you for that.'

'What do you mean by that?'

'Everyone's judging me and thinking the worst.' Her hands clutched the edges of the table, as if she wanted to overturn it, but she just gripped on for a moment before elaborating. 'I can't believe I'm the other woman.'

Rafiq closed his eyes. Liliana was the only woman who had even come close to his blackened heart, but he did not dare tell her that.

He wanted her close, wanted her here, but that night had been too close for comfort.

He would keep her at a safe distance and so he opened his eyes and answered cooly. 'If they're blaming anyone. I am quite sure it's me.'

'And I'm cross with myself—that I didn't ask more questions. I would never have slept with you if I'd known about Yara.'

'You'd prefer to still be a virgin?'

She shot him a look.

'I'm just asking. You would prefer for that night to never have happened.'

Liliana could feel her cheeks burning, blushing at the memory, and, even now, unable to regret it.

'The fact is we did sleep together and that night…' He paused, watching the burn of her cheeks and recalling the soft feel of her skin. Feeling again the bliss of their one night. And no matter how he tried to be practical and deal with things as he usually would, something had shifted in him. No matter how he'd fought it in recent weeks, he could not get his heart to turn back to cold and empty. It beat higher every time he thought of her, and his heart flooded with warmth when he thought of their night. And so, he let her a little closer 'I don't regret that night, Liliana. It changed things for me, and I am asking if it changed things for you?'

'Of course it changed things…' She took a breath, tried not to let him see the turmoil he had caused her heart. 'I've had my private life splashed across the papers.'

'I'm talking about feelings, Liliana. And believe me, I tend not to talk about them. I didn't plan to see you again.'

She took a sliver of Turkish delight, even if she didn't like it, but it was so pretty, the pink set off with green pistachios. And she didn't want to look at him, didn't want him peeking inside her weak heart. Because when

Rafiq spoke about feelings, when he told her that night had changed things for him, it was not conducive to sensible thoughts.

'You tried to pay me off,' she accused, reminding herself how much it had offended her at the time.

'I wasn't paying you off. I was hoping you would sell the stone, not wear it. When you refused it, I sent the fabrics. I knew you would use them wisely, and I wanted…'

'You wanted me away from Simon.'

'Let me finish.' He pointed his finger in warning. He would accept her disquiet and upset, but he wouldn't have thoughts placed as facts. 'I wanted to help give you the start with your business.'

She screwed closed her eyes and nodded, accepted he hoped that his gift had been an attempt only to free her. 'I know that.' She refused to melt to his charms like the treat she held between fingers. Not expecting much, she took a bite and to her surprise found it delicious.

Seriously so.

'That was supposed to be it, I hoped. When you had accepted my gift we could both move on, but…' Rafiq paused. 'You're distracted.'

'I'm not.' She shook her head, swallowed the sweet. 'I just didn't know I liked Turkish delight.'

'Please listen.'

She was trying not to. His gentle words, the reminders of them, the admission of feelings were doing dangerous things to her heart.

She wanted to be told about a harem, that she must dress for him, dance for him, something, anything that could offend.

Instead, he was prising open her heart. His voice was

quiet and low and there was a tone that demanded her attention.

'We spoke about things that I never have with another.'

She refused to be flattered. 'Well, you shouldn't have been speaking those things with me.'

He spoke over her. 'The day of the ball was the anniversary of Khalid's death, and the only person I wanted to see was you.' He watched the column of her pale throat as she swallowed down a smart return. 'I woke up that morning and…' There was a slight pause. 'I ached for you; I was hard for you.' She put her hands over her ears.

'Please stop.'

He did not. 'I could not stand the thought of you alone and dealing with that creep so I made the decision to go to the ball. I had a ceremony I had to go to, and a luncheon to attend, but for the first time that day was made bearable, knowing that by night I would see you.' His admission was unrelenting, 'And last night, even with all that is going on, when my helicopter approached, I felt better knowing you were here.' It made her breathless and a little giddy. 'I believe you missed me too.'

There were tears in her eyes and she felt as if her nose might run, and she did not know how to lie anymore, or to deny what was plainly true. 'You know that I did!' she shouted. Then she rather lamely added, 'But not anymore.'

'You really are a terrible liar.' He gave her a small sympathetic smile for her effort. 'We could have more of that,' Rafiq said. 'Still see each other and be together, but the rules are complicated here.'

'Oh, I doubt it.' Liliana looked back at him. 'In fact, I'm quite sure they all boil down to the same thing—do right.' She took a breath, made herself ask, 'If neither of you want this marriage, then why not simply refuse?'

He didn't answer.

How could he tell her that if this agreement officially ended, as well as the perceived insult, Yara might well have to marry someone else?

She saw his eyes shutter.

'It's not just your parents who want this,' Liliana said more gently than she felt, but she could see he struggled. 'Is it?'

Silence was his answer.

'Is it?'

He opened his eyes then and met her own, and it was like meeting each other again, knowing each other again…

The rules she'd sworn she'd live by were becoming blurry now. It hadn't just been the villagers that had judged her mother harshly; Liliana knew she had too. Yet now she sat opposite a man who, if he so much as crooked his finger, she would find hard to resist. And if she was having a baby…

Oh, she understood her mother so much better now.

And it terrified her.

'The night of the ball I was going to tell you about Yara, and how if I marry, then it must be to her.'

If.

A tiny word that lacerated.

'I had something I wanted to ask you.'

To be his mistress, she was quite sure. And she didn't want to hear it, because then she had to say no. Liliana wanted to lie to herself for just a little while more.

Wanted to wish that they might somehow work. 'I don't want to talk about it right now.'

'Very well.'

Perhaps he too was avoiding things, because instead of attempting to continue the impossible conversation he seemed relieved to leave it for now.

'Do you want me to show you around?'

'Fatima already did that.'

'Good, then would you like to see my crazy pink horse?'

And suddenly she smiled and it was as if for a second they were back to that first night and the magic, for she nodded. 'I would like that very much.'

'Get changed,' he suggested, 'There will be some casual robes, or maybe some jodhpurs.'

'Rafiq,' Liliana cut in. 'I am not borrowing another woman's clothes.'

'You're being ridiculous.'

'Clothes are my thing, Rafiq. They make me, me.'

'Fair enough. Do you want to try something of mine?'

She looked up at six foot three of sheikh and shook her head. 'I'll be fine.'

The jewelled slippers were not suitable for outside, and she attempted to tie on some flat leather sandals, but the straps kept unravelling.

'Not like that…' Rafiq said with an edge and went to pull a rope to summon Fatima.

'Please don't,' Liliana snapped. 'I am capable of tying up my own shoes.'

'Ah, just as you were capable of standing on the tube…' Somehow it brought them both back to the day they had met. For a moment, he was the kind man who had stood to offer her a seat.

And she was Liliana, accepting she had perhaps been a bit brusque.

'Allow me,' he said and, rather than summoning the maid, he knelt. 'You put your feet in…' He guided the sole of her foot, and then crisscrossed the straps and then pulled them tighter around the ankles. 'They need to go up your calf, to your knee.'

His fingers were light, and Liliana stood holding her breath, feeling the *hatta*, his scarf, dust her calf. But more, she recalled the time he had slid down her knickers, and how she had leaned on his shoulders.

'The other foot,' Rafiq said, taking it and guiding it in, trying and failing not to notice just how soft the soles of her feet were, like a kitten who had never been outside.

She jerked a little as he tied the strap behind her knee.

'I'm going to have a crisscross tan,' she said as he stood.

'No,' he said, and reached for a pale robe that he told her belonged to Fatima. 'You wouldn't last five minutes out there.'

Then he wrapped her head in a scarf and arranged it around her neck and she stared ahead, trying not to look up, trying not to breathe.

Trying so hard not to want him still.

The horses were so beautiful and she leaned on the fence of the corral watching two silver ones being put through their paces. They weren't just incredible colours; he told her about their stamina, necessary for the distances and the arid terrain. They walked around his yard, and she was clearly used to horses, for she let them nuzzle and stroked them gently.

'Do you ride?' he asked.

'I used to when I was little, when my father still paid for some things…' She shrugged. 'I haven't ridden in a long time.'

'We could go for a small ride if you like,' he offered.

Though tempted, she shook her head. 'Not in this skirt.'

'Take it off,' Rafiq said, then his voice went gruff. 'Or pull it up.'

'No, thank you.'

In truth she would love to ride, to fling off her skirt that was biting in, but horses were big, and fast, and she wasn't sure if she should be riding if she was… She refused to let herself even think about a baby while he was near. She turned. 'Where's the pink one you promised? I still don't believe you.'

'Still you tease.' Rafiq smiled. 'My groom is just bringing him out.'

'What's his name?'

'Nushiravan, though I call him Nushi. It means "eternal soul", but it also speaks of his majesty, and his streak of rebellion.'

And out he stamped and for a moment all trouble was forgotten. Oh, he was utterly stunning, and yes, there was a pink hue to him.

'He's very contrary,' Liliana said, watching him stamp but also whicker in delight at the sight of his master, and then make his bold way over…

'Like you.'

She could only laugh, because she did not compare to this magnificent, masculine beast.

Yet to Rafiq she did. He thought her beyond beautiful, and delicate yet strong, and he thought her talented and clever, for he was still dwelling on what she'd said about 'do right' and he thought her lively and lovely and so many things.

But she could never be loved.

At least not by him.

And it wasn't just because of the arrangement with Yara, or that his people would never accept Liliana as his bride.

Rafiq knew he was incapable of the depth she would demand as a lover or wife. He did not want his heart to be turned.

But that did not stop him from wanting her.

His mistress she would be.

They spent time with the horses, and he told her about his hopes for the yard, and how he lived between worlds. Not just London and here, but there was the palace and the demands of his position both here and internationally.

They walked away from the yard and the tent, across the sands, but not without direction, for he took her to a rocky overhang, and they sat in its shadow to avoid the midday glare.

'I'm taking these off.' She undid the sandals. 'I think I'm getting a blister.' She massaged her foot for a moment, then took a drink from the flask they were sharing. The water was so cool and refreshing and then he took from his robes a cloth and handed it to her…

She unwrapped it and there were slices of the treat she'd been enjoying this morning.

'How did you know?' She smiled and then it wavered.

He just knew.

She ate the Turkish delight and then lay back and wondered how, when really her world was in chaos, she could know this moment of deep peace.

'Did you used to run here?' she asked, looking over to where he sat, close enough to touch. 'Or was it too hot?'

'I loved training out here.' He looked out, a smile softening his stern mouth. 'The sand made my muscles work harder and the heat gave me an edge.' He gave a silent laugh. 'By the time I got to the track I felt as if I could fly.'

'What about now?'

'I'm not interested.'

She didn't quite believe him, had heard the slightly wistful tone when he'd spoken about training out here.

'Anyway, I'm too old.'

She laughed and moved her foot to give him a little tap, then stopped herself.

He saw it though.

Tried to ignore how it made him feel and got back to talking about running. 'Sprinters peak mid to late twenties…' He could ignore the proximity of her leg no longer.

'You could still run though,' she said, 'just for the…' His hand was on her lower calf, just lightly, and she could pull her foot away, but did not, though her calf was almost knotted with tension resisting herself. 'Just for the pleasure.'

'Yes.'

He moved, picked up both of her feet and placed them in his lap.

'I hate having my feet touched,' she warned because it was true. 'I have to grit my teeth for pedicures and such.'

'Shh,' he told her and got to gentle work.

She looked out, to the sun high in the blue, blue sky and the blinding gold of the dunes and she was not gritting her teeth. Instead she was gripping on to the shifting sand by her side.

'Why do you fight me?' he asked. 'Even now, you pull back from my touch.'

She said nothing.

'You never pulled back when we were together that time.'

'Things were less complicated then. I thought we were two single adults.'

'We are.'

'But not for much longer,' she said, gazing up to meet his eyes. 'I know you're softening me up.'

'What does that mean?'

'I know you're going to marry Yara.' They were staring at each other. 'And I know,' she said, 'that it doesn't stop you wanting me.'

Rafiq liked her directness. 'Our ways are complex,' he said, his fingers or thumbs pressing into her soles quite firmly. 'I remember looking forward to learning about the sex edicts.'

'What are they?'

'Rules,' he said, carrying on the massage. 'Khalid laughed, he warned me I'd be disappointed.'

Odd, but out here, with Liliana, he could speak more

freely about his brother. It made him want her here more. 'I asked him if he thought our father had a mistress.'

'Does he?'

'I wouldn't know,' Rafiq said. 'There are a lot of rules on discretion…' He pressed his thumbs in and wasn't sure if it was pleasure or pain that pinched her expression.

Both.

The pleasure of his touch.

The pain of his words.

She was pulling her feet back, her thighs shaking a little.

No pedicure had ever done this!

He pulled her a little closer, her feet high on his lap, her toes aching to curl, to press into the robe.

And she just lay there, listening to the urging of his words, to just relax, to give in.

'If he does have a lover,' Rafiq said, 'I'm sure she is treated beautifully.'

She pulled her feet back, denying the damp and the pulse between her legs. 'And I'm quite sure your mother hates it.'

This time, Liliana tied her own straps.

They made their slow way back, and with the tent in sight really all she'd found out was the depth of her want, but it just wasn't enough.

He, the most beautiful, sexy, incredible man, wasn't enough.

Not for her needy heart.

She knew that.

But she would try one more time.

Try to get closer before she must leave.

'What did you mean that night?' She knew it was a touchy subject. 'When you said Khalid betrayed you.'

His stride faltered. Rafiq, a trained warrior, showed how much her question had swiped him.

It felt as if they were back in bed, when his hand had paused mid-stroke, when she'd worked out he'd given up running when Khalid had died.

'You don't ask that.'

'Why not?' she said. 'I'm sure there are things you're planning to ask me. I just want to know what happened, how you escaped.'

Rafiq resumed walking, completely comfortable ignoring her question. 'Rafiq.' Liliana stopped, hating how he chose only parts of his life to share with her. Omitting the important parts. Yara, his captivity, whatever had happened with Khalid.

'Rafiq?'

'You don't ask questions like that uninvited.'

'Oh, yes, I do!' She would not be shut down. 'You're different here.'

'Of course I am different. Liliana, there are things I shall never talk about, and what happened during my capture is one of them.'

'What sort of a relationship is that?'

'I told you on the night we met that I don't do relationships.'

'Why am I here then?' she demanded, anger making her bold. 'Why not just tuck me away in a hotel until it was sorted?'

'You're here because we like each other's company, because I think, that despite obstacles, we could be together at times.'

'So just sex?'

'I didn't say that.'

'Yes, you did, you just said you'll never talk about certain topics, never let me get close…'

'I don't do all that.'

'But you did that night.'

'Enough!' he shouted.

'But Rafiq, surely…' She reached for his hand, grabbed his arm, desperate for him not to shut the conversation down, but he pulled back, looked down.

'You were right,' he said, taking her back to their first night. 'You are annoying.'

Yes, that was cruel, yes, that took away the sweetness of their conversation where she had skipped by his side, trying to make him smile, but it was better than let her get too close.

Love was dangerous.

It was by far too dangerous.

For months he'd been engineering this and finally the moment was here.

More than weak, barely able to walk, they had made it to the car...

'Where's the blanket to cover the crown prince?' He could hear Balach talking to his wife, his voice panicked. 'Give me your wrap to cover him.'

'Are you sure we can trust him, Balach?' she asked her husband, taking the wrap from her shoulders.

For the first time Rafiq saw the baby.

She was tiny. Painfully thin with sunken cheeks, her complexion was dusky and she lay limp in her mother's arms.

'Of course we can trust him,' Balach said. 'He is going to take care of us. He gave us his word...'

There was barely anything in Rafiq's stomach but he thought he would throw up.

Oh, and this attempt to escape was by far too dangerous.

'Get in,' Balach said. 'Stay quiet, especially at the border.'

He was in the trunk, covered in a wrap that would do nothing if the trunk was opened at the border and they all knew it.

The car bounced over bumps as they neared the bridge and they knew they would be stopped to show their papers, but if they went to open the trunk...

Rafiq had told Balach to just drive through the hail of bullets.

He'd hoped that way there'd be a chance to live.

Now he'd seen the baby...

They were both silent as the sun slid behind the desert abode and the oil lamps were lit.

Both angry.

Both wanting.

The low table had been set and candles had been lit, and when she walked into the seraglio, she saw a deep red velvet gown that Fatima had laid out for her, as well as flowers placed on her pillow.

Then music filled the tent, and it was sensual and low, and she lived again for a few seconds the dance they had shared at the ball. Barely touching, but so into each other. Even days later the memory took her breath away.

And she was not going to sleep with him here.

On that Liliana was decided.

She'd meant what she said about not turning into her mother, and while Yara hung over them, she would not be sleeping with Rafiq.

As well as that, she was worried she was starting to show.

That Rafiq's knowing eyes would pick up on the changes to her body.

But even without Yara or the baby, there was something bigger troubling her. Rafiq didn't want a relationship in the same way she did. He didn't like entanglement. And with every passing moment she felt as if he drew her closer into his golden web, and yet she had to prise out details.

Rafiq seemed to think he could ask about her, know any given thought.

She wasn't allowed though to get too close to him.

She came out of the seraglio just as he was on the way to his sleeping area and he frowned when he saw her.

'Do you need Fatima?'

'Need Fatima?'

'Just pull the cord in the bathroom.'

'Why?' She frowned, knowing damn well what he meant. He was off to change for dinner and clearly expected her to do the same.

Well, she'd meant what she said about not choosing from the selection of robes, and more to the point she didn't quite trust her own willpower tonight. Rafiq was looking sinfully sexy, all unshaven and moody, and perhaps it might be more sensible to take dinner in the seraglio.

And leave tomorrow.

She'd been right that first night.

Liliana was on the very edge of telling him her truth, that she was scared she might be pregnant, scared what that might mean for them…

He picked up a handful of grapes and ate them from the bunch and somehow made it look sexy.

'Pips,' he said and ran his tongue between his teeth and God help her it made her stomach feel weak. 'I am going to bathe,' Rafiq told her. 'How about you?'

'Pardon?' She startled, and then realised he wasn't asking her to join him.

'We shall be eating soon, and you need to change.'

'What happened to the man I met and his impeccable manners? Am I not tidy enough for you?'

'No, you're not. You're wearing the same clothes that you had on yesterday,' Rafiq said, 'and not only have we been at the stables and walking all day, but frankly, you look uncomfortable. I want you to enjoy dinner…' He gave her a thin, somewhat impatient smile. 'So shall I call Fatima for you?'

'Am I to go to the Chamber of Adornment and ready myself for you?'

'No.' Rafiq came over. 'Because you've made it very clear you don't want sex. If anything, you seem determined to pick a fight.' He might have seen her go a little red, because she was certain there was a hint of a triumphant smile as he voiced her thoughts. 'Is that so you can flounce off to bed?'

'No,' she lied, even though that had been her plan.

'Wash or don't wash,' he told her. 'Dress however you want. You are beautiful whatever you choose to do.'

She bit her bottom lip from a smart retort; he could be so bloody rude and also so kind, all with the same words.

He headed off to bathe and she sat there, her skirt digging into her, and all hot and bothered, and of course it was a relief to head to the Diwan Al-Zayn.

It would seem she didn't require an *everything* night… A deep bath had been drawn and it was wonderful to slip off her clothes. There was an angry red mark where her skirt had dug into her waist, and somehow, she knew that her skirt would not be going back on.

Was it possible to be bigger than this morning?

Slipping into the bath, she felt a dreadful knot of anxiety. Really, she didn't need to do the test to know she was pregnant.

She felt scared to be here.

Nervous of Rafiq finding out and with no clue as to what his reaction might be.

She closed her eyes and breathed in the fragrant water.

There was no question—she would be keeping the baby. The very real question Liliana was asking herself was whether Rafiq had to know.

She didn't want the hell of custody battles and really what chance would she have against a crown prince?

Or worse, if he simply wanted no part in their child's life.

Liliana herself had lived the agony of that.

She sat up in the bath, anxious because these thoughts of a baby, their baby, were making it feel real.

And she could not afford to think like that here.

Wrapping a *hammam* towel around herself, she went out to get dressed, then cursed herself for rinsing her bra and knickers out. She didn't have many options but she'd be damned if she was wearing that red velvet gown, and instead pulled on the muslin nightdress.

She reached for a shawl from the bed and wrapped it around her shoulders and headed out.

Stepping into the lounge, she walked to the screened area and there was Rafiq, dressed exquisitely in a silver robe, the evening shadow on his jaw, far darker than one day's worth, but beautifully trimmed. He really had dressed for dinner and looked every inch the crown prince he was.

'I was right,' Rafiq said as she lowered herself onto a cushion opposite him. 'You look beautiful whatever you wear.'

'Thank you.'

'I shall just say this and leave it there,' Rafiq told her.

'Go ahead.'

'Your nightdress is see-through when you stand.'

'Thank you for letting me know.'

'Of course.'

She really was completely underdressed because this meal truly was an occasion, though perhaps Rafiq ate like this all the time. The mezze was served on a copper-and-ceramic dish and Rafiq spoke her through the delicacies. There were pillowy flatbreads and she helped herself to some baba ganoush with pomegranate seeds, and a dolma, then her hand hovered over a small pastry.

'*Fateyah*,' Rafiq explained. 'Filled with labneh.'

'What's that?'

'A cheese, very creamy.'

Were pregnant women allowed to eat cheese? She pulled her hand away and had another dolma instead.

* * *

At first, she wouldn't meet his eyes.

But even mildly arguing, for Rafiq there was more real conversation at this table than there had been anywhere else in his life. And even mildly arguing there was the odd smile and the meeting of eyes, and a togetherness, even if they sat apart and were both a little cross or frustrated or whatever this latest emotion that had surfaced was.

There was this bittersweet feeling, a certain warmth, even if they bristled a touch. Togetherness, for there was a slight smile of thanks from her as he served her the main course—grilled quail with saffron.

'Try the sumac salad,' he suggested, and she nodded.

'Thanks.'

He topped up her drink.

Addressed it. 'I've offended you.'

'Yes,' she admitted. 'You seem to think we can resume things, be together again, yet you offer less than you did that night. In fact, you regret telling me the things you did.'

'That night was an exception,' Rafiq said. 'That night I wasn't a crown prince.'

She frowned.

'That night…' They had both shed their skins, and he did not know how best to say that. 'Boundaries were crossed. We were anonymous then.'

'But we weren't,' she refuted. 'I showed you exactly who I was—I told you I didn't know how to hide when I was with you. How is that anonymous, Rafiq?'

He could be cruel; she was about to find out.

'It was a hook-up.' He looked right at her as he said it. 'I put on a persona.'

Perhaps he expected her to gasp, or burst into tears, but even with her lack of experience, Liliana knew it had been far more than that.

'So do you tell all your hook-ups about Khalid betraying you?'

'Leave it.'

'No.' She shook her head. 'I'm curious.' She leaned forward, the shawl sliding from her shoulders as they met face to face. 'Do you give all your lovers a little snippet? If we all met up, could we join up the story of your life?'

He met her angry gaze, his beautiful mouth a little surly as she won this argument.

Not that he would admit it.

'Liliana, maybe in time I might…' He shrugged.

'We don't have time, Rafiq,' she told him. 'I have a life. I need to be back at work.'

He fixed her with his glare, the one that could stop asteroids, except she reached for her goblet and took a sip, then angrily put it down.

'Okay, maybe I was insensitive about Khalid, but do you know what I don't get? The bit I can't work out—why are you so beholden to Yara?'

'I am not beholden.'

'Rubbish,' she snapped. 'Her uncle kept you a prisoner, her country is responsible for the death of your brother, you have every reason to refuse this marriage.' Hot tears were spilling down her cheeks, but they didn't embarrass her because they were angry ones. Tears of pure fury. 'I can only assume that you do actually love her and I am being fed more lies.'

'No. Yara has her career. I don't want to be tied to anyone, and politically it makes sense.'

'Politically.' She made a scoffing noise.

'It matters,' he responded. 'You have this romantic notion about marriage, when it is more a business transaction. That is why the edicts allow for lovers. They protect the wife. That is why we got in trouble—we were seen in public twice.'

'That's forbidden?'

'Strictly.'

'So, we couldn't be seen out.' Her lips moved into an incredulous, utterly mirthless smile. 'Or would I be passed off as one of your staff.'

'We would *never* be seen together.'

Wow.

He did not mince words.

'I shan't be showering Yara with affection, believe me. I offer you everything except one day being queen.'

'No, you offer me a life of being second, of being the other family, of watching you with your chosen one.' Her eyes narrowed. 'You don't want love.' She could see it. 'You don't want it from Yara, from me, from anyone.'

'Correct,' he said, 'I don't.'

'Then I don't want this conversation. In fact I think tomorrow I should fly home.'

'Liliana,' he shouted. 'We need to talk.'

'No,' she said, making her way to her chamber, but he walked behind her. 'I don't want the crumbs you offer, and I don't want you.'

'Liar.'

He caught her.

'That last one was a lie, because you do want me.' He

held her shoulders to turn her around to face him, but she resisted, for she knew she would meet his kiss. 'I will take care of you, more than take care of you.'

His hands moved down her ribs, to her hips, again to turn her around, but still she resisted, though not his touch. She could feel the raw passion, knew that in a moment the nightdress would be off and those knowing eyes and skillful hands would roam her body. Oh, she knew that, for she wanted it desperately too.

He had awoken in her this want and thick desire and she did not know how to douse it, and now she too ached for more of what they had. So instead of turning, stripping, she pressed back into his erection.

'You are bold,' he said, kissing her neck, pulling her in.

'You made me bold,' she said, for she wanted him urgently and knew if she took off her nightgown there would be yet another conversation to have.

He went to turn her again, to kiss her, to strip her before him, but still she resisted, too nervous to expose her ripening body to what those knowing eyes might see.

And so, she knelt for him, facing away as he pushed her nightdress up, and he moaned when he saw her naked bottom.

Her knickers were still hung by the wash area, but that was irrelevant; she just felt the primal need as he explored her cheeks and then came the sound of him unbelting and his robes lifting and then the bliss of his fingers checking she was moist, and the warm cup of his hand on her mound…

For both, the thought of having no contraception flashed through their minds.

Liliana decided it was too late anyway and it didn't matter now.

For Rafiq, the thought was the same; it didn't matter now. Here in the desert, naked and unsheathed, it didn't matter. He squeezed in, for the first time unsheathed, and he revelled in the new sensation as over and over he sank into her. He had been her first, they had obstacles, yes, but there was no question in his mind she was now his.

Liliana felt the grip of his hands as he moved her a little, then he knelt up higher, pushed her nightdress up to her neck and for a moment, his hand rested on the base of her spine and she knew he was watching them.

She sank lower, resting her head now on her arms and while taut with arousal, somehow limp as he moved her, just loving the feel of him, and then he moved faster and she felt the final swell and then a shout from Rafiq that had her pulse and tighten and close her eyes as her body released.

'Liliana,' he said as he pulled out and his hand was back, cupping her again, somehow soothing where she was tender. 'I'll take care of you now.'

She lay, bottom up and a little embarrassed at how easily, how quickly this man could bring her to her knees, and expose a different side of her. He went to slip her nightdress fully off, to take her to bed, but she hastily pulled the flimsy gown down and dashed off to tidy herself up and collect herself.

Her eyes looked shocked when she checked in the mirror. She was flushed and wide-eyed and about to walk through the veils when she had sworn never to.

He changed every facet of her.

For how could she even consider staying when he

had told her he did not want love? Told her that the man she'd met that night had been a persona, that the person she had possibly fallen in love with might not even exist.

And yet she freshened up then covered herself with a wrap and instead of taking the long way around, pulled back the veils to his chamber.

He lay on top of the furs, up on one arm and staring approvingly at her.

'Come here.'

Rafiq would have carried her to his bed and tidied her. Now she seemed shy as she walked towards him and slipped beneath the furs and then threw off the wrap…

'It's warm enough to lie on top,' he said, because the fire was dancing high and he knew merely lying atop the furs would keep them warm, but she shook her head and hid a little, and he thought he knew why. 'I know we didn't use anything,' he said. 'But if there are consequences know that I shall take care of you both.'

Liliana closed her eyes. She had a feeling they were a few months late for this discussion, but she was curious to know.

'What would happen?' she asked, forcing her eyes open to look at him. 'Would your people hate me, would Yara…?'

'Shh,' he reassured. 'I would take care of you. Both of you. I'm sure the people assume I already have children.'

'So, it wouldn't count.'

'Of course it would count,' Rafiq reassured.

'Unofficially though.'

'Of course.' He nodded. 'Liliana,' he said when her eyes filled with tears. 'Surely you can understand that?'

Rafiq hated that she cried.

CHAPTER TEN

RAFIQ LIKED HAVING Liliana in his bed.

Liked the feel of her lying in his arms, the softness of her skin, but he loathed the tears that fell on his chest, even if she tried to hide them.

He had that post-sex clarity, almost the same high that came after a run.

Absolutely he could fix things.

'That shouldn't have happened,' she said.

He gave a low laugh, 'Well, it did.' He reached down and moved her hand from his stomach. 'And if you don't want it happening again, you'd better stop.'

Liliana pulled back her hand. 'I meant, I wanted things to be sorted properly before we slept together. If they can ever be sorted.'

'They can be,' he said far more assuredly than possibly he should. How the hell did he explain his and Yara's situation without betraying Yara? Liliana had gone all shy after they'd had sex and he guessed she felt guilty, when there was absolutely no need for her to be.

Her threat to leave had unsettled him.

What if he promised to be more open, to be more like the man she had met that night?

What if he proved it by opening up now?

That was how much he wanted Liliana in his life, in his bed.

Before he could talk himself out of it, Rafiq spoke up. 'Khalid told them how they could capture me.'

Liliana, whose hand was back playing with the hair on his stomach, froze. She actually held her breath, so scared was she that even that sound might interrupt.

But no.

'There is a tunnel under my home in Belgravia—it used to be less secure than it is now. Only three people knew of its existence. My father, Khalid and me.'

'No-one else?'

'My father insisted that the rebels perhaps had someone follow me, or it had been somehow leaked, but we both know that is not the case.'

'How?'

'My captors told me. At first, I thought they were lying, but from the details they gave…' He shook his head. 'And my father knows it's true, because we cannot talk about it. I know that it kills my father that Khalid did that.' He closed his eyes. 'He'd only been captured a few days when he broke.'

'Poor man.'

Rafiq's eyes widened at her response. He didn't need her sympathy, but shouldn't that be more leaning to *poor you*?

'He was married, wasn't he?'

'Yes.'

'Do you think they blackmailed him, threatened his wife?'

'Probably.'

'You don't think you'd have done the same?'

'Absolutely not. I would never have betrayed my brother.'

'God only knows what he went through.'

'Wild horses wouldn't have dragged it from me.' Rafiq shook his head. 'He wasn't just a brother—he was the crown prince. His death could have ended the lineage.'

'I doubt he was thinking that far ahead,' she suggested. 'How *did* you get out?'

He shook his head.

Wasn't that enough revelation?

But they were in the space they found, the quiet of night, and he wanted her to remain.

If she wanted to be here after hearing this.

'Balach,' he said. 'He was a night guard. He only came in every couple of weeks.'

He told her how he'd watched all the guards, trying to work out the weakest. About Balach's food, and his wife having a baby.

And it did not feel as if he was serving his guts up on a plate.

It was just a slow revelation. He could feel her breath on his chest, and occasionally she moved a touch, rearranged her leg, but as he revealed the darkest parts, he felt somehow lighter.

He told her about the baby needing surgery and his offer to help.

'He said yes?' Liliana checked, anxious to get to the end, to know the baby was okay.

'No,' Rafiq said. 'He said it was too dangerous. There were too many guards and there was also a checkpoint on the bridge to here. They were checking papers, opening car boots...'

'So what did you do?'

'I waited,' Rafiq said, 'but I was getting weak. Soon I wouldn't be able to walk and I told him that. He gave me his meal that night and we spoke. I persuaded him.'

'How?'

'I said it was his baby's best chance. I promised him a new life.' His voice cracked, and she dared not look up, because he would hate her to see him like that.

She wanted to press Fast Forward. To know what happened so she could breathe out in relief and then concentrate. But she was also scared to ask. There was a darkness to Rafiq and she was terrified she might know why.

'He still said no, but he started to tell me a plan. There were two guards on the perimeter,' Rafiq said, having cleared his throat. 'And there was one at the main entrance to the tunnel, but he was lazy, Balach told me. He spent a lot of time on his phone, or away from his post. Time was the biggest danger—the guards changed shift just after sunrise. His baby was getting weaker too. We agreed the next time he was guarding me that we would leave.'

Rafiq thought back; it had been three weeks before Balach had worked again, his body was fading, he barely had strength and he was worried Balach had revealed their plans.

'Then he arrived, and it was time to escape. Balach was right, the guard was lazy, and asleep. We got past the perimeter and his wife was there with the car.' He paused. 'And their baby.'

'She must have been terrified.'

'No, she was very stoic. She told me to get in the trunk—we all knew if they inspected it, we were dead.'

'Were you stopped?'

'There was a border.' He was silent. 'I heard the guards asking for papers. The plan was if they asked him to open the trunk to just drive straight through. Make it to the other side and hope.'

'Were you terrified?'

'I think I was too weak for that. I just…' He closed his eyes, his heart started thumping, and it was not a pleasant feeling, having a heart that beat with emotion and it caused his voice to catch. 'I felt guilt. They were trusting me, and they had a baby. I had told him it would work, that I would make sure of it, and because I am a crown prince he believed in me. The things is, I was using him.'

She lay very still, could hear the rapid beat of his heart and knew he must be reliving it, and she wasn't sure now she wanted to get to the end. 'What happened?' she ventured.

'The guards barely glanced at the papers. They waved us through. I kept waiting for gunshots, yet we were driving. We made it to a safe house.'

And it should be a happy ending, but his voice was so flat.

'The baby?'

'She had surgery a week later, in London. She is still there.'

'Do you see her?'

'No. They have a new life.'

'Surely you would like to see…'

'I doubt they would want to see me. I put them in grave danger.'

'You saved their baby.'

'Perhaps, but that was more luck.' He was honest. 'I manipulated him,' Rafiq said. 'I knew his weakness—his love for his wife and for his child.'

Liliana peeled herself from his body and sat up.

'Love wasn't his weakness—it made him strong,' Liliana said. 'And the same for his wife. It made them brave enough to take the chance.'

It was a different way of looking at it; in fact he hadn't really looked at it that way before. It had been too painful to think about, the guilt as to how it might have turned out too appalling to consider.

Yet despite pushing thoughts aside, of course he had.

Over and over the worst-case scenarios had invaded his mind.

Then her hand closed around him and he felt the softness of her lips.

And there were no more thoughts.

CHAPTER ELEVEN

LILIANA DID NOT regret sleeping with Rafiq, or the very intimate night.

She relieved him with a mouth he slowly tutored and then lay in the dark in his arms and just before he fell asleep, she asked 'If I am pregnant?'

'You'll be fine,' said Mr Arrogant as he patted her arm.

'But if I am?'

'Seriously, you'll be fine. I'll take care of you—surely you know that.'

'But…' She didn't understand. 'If one kiss by a lake causes offence…'

'That was too public.' He thought he was reassuring her. 'As I said, they probably think I am a father already. Seriously, don't worry.'

And she would never be first.

Nor her baby.

And so, the decisions she had made earlier remained.

Tomorrow she would go home.

Rafiq had said that the press were sorted and if not, she would join her mother at the hotel.

But she could not stay.

They would lie here forever, making love, eating Turkish delight off her pregnant stomach.

'What?' he said as she gave a soft laugh at her own thoughts.

'Nothing.'

It could not be like this.

She would be hidden from the world, their baby too.

Her mind was made up; she would tell him about the baby from England.

Rafiq woke first and lay there. For once his mind was quiet and it was because she was here by his side, Rafiq knew.

But the peace would not last.

He could not satisfactorily explain his connection to Yara.

Liliana was clever, too clever—honing in on Yara, asking why he was beholden. Of course he wasn't, but he was bound by Yara's secret.

He thought of many dark days imprisoned, when the secret he held on to could have brought his freedom. Never, even then, had there been any doubt.

He rolled onto his side and looked at Liliana asleep beside him. She lay on her back, one arm stretched out; the other one, close to him, was up on the pillow and he watched the soft rise and fall of her chest.

Then she started to wake, and he watched her lashes struggle to part, and how she seemed to wrestle in protest of waking up or diving back to sleep. She moaned and he watched her stretch.

The fur slipped and he saw the changes in her breasts, a fullness that hadn't been there, and the areola were a darker pink, her nipples swollen and not from his attention. His eyes moved to her exposed stomach, and he breathed out in relief, for there was no bump to see.

Or was there?

He looked at her gorgeous golden curls, her pale flat stomach, and he was tempted to wake her with three words.

Are you pregnant?

It was an obvious question to ask. He thought of that night and the off-brand condoms and he recalled his own unease at the change. And it had not just been once; they had made love many times and of course he'd been careful. But perhaps not quite as careful as he usually would be.

He was indeed reckless when it came to Liliana.

Right now, his head was tightened in horror. The thought of a baby, a real one, a person he must love in his life.

Right now, he was wondering how the hell to juggle this latest ball. How did Liliana feel about this?

Did she even know?

'Hey,' he said when her sleepy eyes finally opened to him and he watched as, rather too quickly, she retrieved the fur and covered herself, like some shy virgin on her wedding night.

Then he recalled her questions deep in the night.

Oh, Liliana knew!

'How did you sleep?' Rafiq asked.

'Very well.' Liliana smiled, but then it faded from her lips as she remembered the decision she had made.

It was the right decision.

Surely?

'Rafiq…'

'Yes.'

'Can I tell you something?'

She watched as he inhaled deeply. 'Yes.'

'I want to go home.'

It was the last thing Rafiq had expected to hear.

He had braced himself to be told about a baby. Instead, her clear blue eyes held his and she told him she wanted to go home.

'I don't think that's a very good idea,' he responded evenly. 'We have a lot to sort out.'

'No,' she refuted, and sat up in the bed. '*You* have a lot to sort out—you and Yara, and until that's sorted…' She shook her head and then took a breath, perhaps arguing with herself. 'It's not just that.'

'You can tell me.' He gently touched her back as he did when she was upset. 'Please tell me what's on your mind.'

Was he really so unapproachable, even to the person he'd been the most open with?

Rafiq thought of what Yara had said, how she wouldn't feel able to tell him her secret if it was now. And he thought too about the slightly mocking headlines beneath the photos of Liliana, which had thankfully all been taken down, but they had expressed surprise that the crown prince might actually have feelings after all.

'I have to go, because every day, every night that I stay, I become more of your mistress.'

'I've told you,' he said as patiently as he could, 'they cannot force me to marry.'

'It's not a solution though, is it, because it would cause great offence if you were to marry me. Am I right?'

'Correct.'

'And so I'd be tucked away.'

'Hardly tucked away. You would have a residence in the grounds of the palace…' His mind flashed to the edicts. 'We could be together in London.' He looked at her clear blue eyes and he trusted them, and there was a secret he could share, not the one he'd sworn to keep, but surely it might help. 'You can't tell anyone this, but Yara's father is ill.'

'Okay.' She shrugged impatiently. 'I'm rather tired of hearing her name every time we speak about us.'

'I get that, but listen, he is very ill. That's the reason she was in London—to tell me. She knew things were coming to a head.' Those blue eyes simply waited for him to reveal more. 'Perhaps in a couple of years' time it will be easier for you and I to be together.'

'When her father has died?' she checked, and he nodded.

'Her father is the one who is pushing for marriage.'

'So I have to wait for a man to die for us to be together?' She shook her head. 'Marriage or not, you and Yara share something, a bond, a promise, sex, I don't quite know what. But I am not going to stay hidden, I shall never be your mistress. I simply refuse to be.'

'I am not sleeping with Yara.'

'I believe my father used to say the same to my mother,' she angrily retorted. 'Don't tell me you are not like my father and don't tell me the circumstances are different, because right now it feels the same.'

She pulled the fur up tightly around her. 'Rafiq, you promised me that I could leave at any time.'

Only that was before and this was now, and she was going to leave without telling him.

'I did,' he reluctantly agreed and then he looked at the person he trusted the most, and swore that one day she would trust him enough to reveal her truth. 'I shall make the arrangements.'

Rafiq really was a man of his word because a short while later he came into the lounge where she was dressed in the clothes she'd arrived in and seated on a cushion by the seraglio.

'The plane is being readied, and the helicopter will take you to the airport in an hour or so.'

'Aren't you coming to see me off?' she said, while knowing they could not be seen together again.

'You know I can't.' He sat down beside her, 'Liliana, I think your leaving is a really bad idea. We can talk uninterrupted here.'

'And sleep together.' She turned to him. 'I don't have a cast iron heart like you, Rafiq. Every time we sleep together, I'm…' She paused, scared to tell him the true depth of her feelings, scared that she was stuck loving a prince who could never deeply commit or sustain her needy heart.

Such a needy heart.

She did not want to go back to eager smiles and fighting for attention.

'Every time we sleep together, I become more entangled,' she explained. 'And that's something that you don't really want.'

'I am trying…' He looked over. 'I know I keep people

at a distance. I know I'm different to the man you first met. I'll be Mr Nice Guy…'

'I like both of you,' she admitted. 'But if I stay here, I'm going to break a promise to myself. And I don't want to do that. Don't make this hard for me. Please.'

This parting was the hardest.

She felt as if she were choking in an effort not to cry, and though he didn't want her to go, he didn't seem cross. Instead when the helicopter arrived, he held her for a full moment.

'You're not annoying,' he said. 'You're cute.'

'Thank you,' she sniffed and half laughed, clinging on to him. 'But I need more.'

'Call me,' he said. 'Anytime. For anything.'

'Thank you.'

'I mean it,' Rafiq said. 'We can talk anything through. There's nothing that you can't tell me.'

'I only wish you felt the same.'

She was so uncertain if she was right to be leaving, even now. She had to peel herself from his arms and fight the urge to simply stay. But all too soon she was on the helicopter, torn with indecision.

She had been so close to telling him about the baby.

So close.

Rafiq did not come out to see the helicopter, and not just because of discretion.

He could not.

There was the crushing weight of emotion and he sat on the cushion outside the seraglio, his elbows on his knees, head in hands.

How could he let her leave, but then how could he demand she stay?

He felt as close to despair as he had the day he had found out Khalid had died.

As if a part of his soul had left his body.

And that was about Liliana.

He could not even begin to get his head around the idea of a baby.

Unless he was imagining things, unless she wasn't pregnant after all? Surely she'd have told him.

Surely she knew she could.

'Sir?'

Rafiq frowned at the sound of his security guard's voice and then looked up.

'Salar?'

'I don't know if I should be mentioning this. If you want it to just go ahead…'

'Mention what?'

Salar could not acknowledge he had seen Liliana; was that why he appeared so uncomfortable?

'It's fine,' Rafiq said.

'I just can't imagine I'd want my…' He paused. 'Princess Yara.'

'Just tell her no. I don't want to see anyone today.' Certainly he did not want Yara crying and pleading they marry.

But that was not Yara's intention, it would seem.

'Do you know about the airside meeting?' Salar asked.

'What meeting?'

'Princess Yara has arranged a VIP lounge, airside.'

'With?'

Oh, God, no wonder Salar looked uncomfortable; who would want the women in their lives meeting to speak?

Not that Yara was in his life, but Salar didn't know that.

But worse than that, far worse than that, was the thought of Liliana coming face to face with Yara.

Not because he had anything to hide. In fact, he hoped Yara was going to confide in Liliana.

No, the dread was for Liliana, and her reaction when she opened the door and found Yara waiting.

'Arrange a helicopter,' Rafiq ordered. 'Now. And get me airside.'

He'd get onto a plane if he had to.

There were strict controls to get through.

Yara would have flown in from Al-Nawar, but technically, while she remained airside, there would be no immigration, no record of her entering Al-Zahir.

This meeting never took place.

CHAPTER TWELVE

THE HELICOPTER LANDED and Liliana was taken to a building on the tarmac.

'If I could have your passport, madam?'

'Of course.'

There was no lining up at customs in Rafiq's world. No feeding your passport into reluctant machines, or trying to find where to look at the camera. All that was quietly and discreetly dealt with.

There was no luggage, and in her far too tight skirt and her mother's blouse and awful wedges, she must look quite a sight, but the attendant was far too polished to raise even the edge of her eyebrow.

'The plane is just fuelling,' the helpful attendant explained as she walked her through to airside. 'It should be about an hour.'

'Thank you.'

'I'll come and knock when the captain is ready for you,' said the attendant, opening up a door but not stepping in, just gesturing for Liliana to follow through.

And then Liliana realised why the attendant could not so much as step in.

A woman stood looking out of the window, and she turned and gave a tight smile as Liliana stood stunned.

'Please,' she said, 'close the door.'

She did so. 'Princess Yara.'

Yara was stunning,

She was draped in willow-green velvet, and had long, ebony hair that fell into curls, and it was completely overwhelming, worse than when she'd opened the door to her father's wife.

'Princess Yara, I would like to apologise...' She paused, and only then did she notice there was another woman to the side, kneeling on a cushion with her head bowed. 'If I had known that you and Rafiq, I mean Prince Rafiq...' It really was impossible, but Yara nodded as if she accepted this conversation was indeed difficult.

'Shall we sit?' Yara suggested, and sat in front of her maiden, and Liliana took a seat opposite, grateful for the moment to gather herself.

She felt Yara's eyes take in her outfit, and her blink of surprise when she saw her shoes, then she spoke.

'It is a delicate situation.' Yara paused for such a long moment, and Liliana didn't know if it was an invitation to speak.

And she could not bear the silence. 'I really am so sorry, I was appalled when I found...'

'Please.' Yara put up her hand to halt the slight tirade. 'I am not here for an apology.' She hesitated for another long moment and it would seem this very composed woman just did not know what to say, but then finally she spoke. 'What has Rafiq told you?'

Liliana frowned. 'He didn't tell me about you—that's the point.'

'I meant, what has he told you since?'

Liliana glanced at the maiden, unsure how much she

could say, and if she even wanted to reveal conversations between herself and Rafiq.

'You can speak freely in front of Jasmine. Please, tell me what Rafiq has said.'

'Not very much,' Liliana answered, but Yara raised her brows in a gesture of disbelief.

'That there is pressure from your families.'

'Yes,' Yara said and there was another long pause. This time Liliana didn't fill it. 'Did Rafiq tell you I am a botanist?'

'No.'

'Of course not, Rafiq would have no interest. I spend hours on my drawings. I have to go on trips to observe my beloved veiled orchid.' She gave a slight helpless shrug. 'Can you imagine discussing flowers with Rafiq?' She gave a little laugh, a small ironic laugh which seemed to invite Liliana to nod and agree.

Except she could not, because her answer was 'Yes.' For indeed she could imagine discussing flowers with Rafiq. He had looked at her fashion sketches, and they had spoken all day about his passion for horses. 'Yes,' she said again, 'if flowers were my passion, then I could picture discussing them with him.'

Yara closed her eyes. Clearly this wasn't going well, and there was another awful stretch of silence.

A dreadfully long stretch and, uninvited, Liliana filled it. 'I shan't be his mistress. I've already told Rafiq that.'

'Prince Rafiq,' Yara corrected.

Liliana felt her lips tighten, and she wanted to correct the princess, because if they were ever going to get anywhere then surely they had to drop the titles. She glanced to the handmaiden, wishing Yara would ask her to leave, but she just sat silently behind Yara, her hands resting in her lap.

'Neither Prince Rafiq nor I want this marriage,' Yara finally said. 'The reason I was in London was to tell him that there was more pressure from my family.'

'I see.'

There came a moment of relief, for Rafiq had not really been lying—well, not outright—and then the relief was removed when Yara next spoke.

'I asked him to create a scandal.'

Liliana looked up. So too did her maiden, as if surprised by what Princess Yara had just said. 'A scandal?'

'I engineered this.' Yara nodded, confirming her choice of words. 'I wanted an excuse to delay the marriage. So, you see, Rafiq did nothing wrong…'

'Really?' Liliana offered a rather sarcastic response, dropping titles now, truly not caring, because finding out she had been a pawn in whatever games these two were playing really was the final straw.

'I just wanted to clear things up. Rafiq is an honourable man. He was not cheating on me. There is no reason for you to apologise, and no reason for either of us to be cross…'

Liliana could have offered another cheeky 'really' but she had no more to say, and certainly she would not cry here.

'I'm pleased to have cleared things up,' Yara said, and her voice was a little shaky and Liliana realised the princess was also on the edge of tears. She stood, ending the odd meeting, and for a moment Yara looked faint, as if she might have to sit straight back down, but her maiden helped her out from the greeting room.

Liliana was too stunned to even stand, but she did turn her head as they left and saw the maiden's hand lightly touch Yara's back. And in that second, she knew the two women were lovers.

It was the same touch she had given Rafiq that first night when she'd first seen his scars. That slight touch of support, if that was the right word, that moment of acknowledging the one you love's pain.

Yes, love.

And it was then she accepted fully that she loved Rafiq, and that was why she could spend a day discussing pink horses with him. She loved him now, as she had loved him then.

As Yara did her maiden.

Or whoever Jasmine really was.

Yet, she'd been used all along.

Liliana hated what she'd found out. It had all felt so natural that night; that was what she'd loved about them…only it hadn't been. Rafiq had been telling the truth when he'd said he had invented a persona. He had smiled into her eyes, said all she wanted to hear as they kissed for the camera.

She felt both angry and used.

And when those feelings remained, when they would not quieten or calm, when she sat airside, neither here nor there, the door opened and the most complex, best-looking bastard in the world—and the father of her baby, if indeed she was pregnant—stood there.

'Liliana, I came as soon as I found out…' For the first time she didn't have to fight the instinct to run to him. Instead she fought not to slap him. 'I had no idea Jasmine was going to do this.'

He'd met Yara on her way out, seen her crying, and for a moment he was sure she'd told Liliana her truth, and was so grateful.

'Yara…'

'I had to know for myself that you hadn't told her…'

'I haven't.'

'I came here to, I wanted to for you, I tried, but I'm sorry Rafiq, I couldn't do it.'

That cold, slow-beating heart must have warmed a touch, because he actually felt the descent in his chest of a sinking heart as Yara cried. 'I told her I was not cross, that you are an honourable man.' She was sobbing. 'But I could not tell her…'

'It's okay,' Rafiq said.

They were standing on the tarmac and no doubt giving the ground staff hives at this very forbidden meeting, and so he nodded and walked off, and one of the staff gestured to the door.

Behind which was Liliana.

'Thank you,' Rafiq said.

He stepped in and she looked up, her face as white as porcelain and anger blazing in her eyes. She didn't seem to want to hear that he'd had no idea Yara would arrange this.

'You used me.' She stood and walked towards him, and if he were not warrior trained, he might have been tempted to step back. 'You used me,' she said again, pointing at him with her finger.

'What are you talking about?'

'Yara wanted a scandal and so you manufactured one.'

'No!' He was tempted to run out of the VIP suite and yank Yara back, but really what was the point? 'I did not use you for even a second. I told Yara no when she requested a scandal.'

'Liar,' she accused. 'Yara would do anything to stop it getting out about her and Jas—'

She had never been scared of Rafiq before, not when he'd pulled her into a car, nor when he'd fixed her with a glare.

Not even now, when he pushed a hand over her mouth and moved her to the wall.

'Shh.' He warned and wide-eyed she nodded, realising that her voice might have been rather loud. 'Speak quietly.' He moved his hand away, but his face remained so close she could feel his breathing. 'Yara told you?' His voice was an incredulous whisper. 'She just told me she couldn't bring herself to.'

'She didn't *have* to tell me. Of course they're together. Anyone could see it…' She saw concern flash across his features. 'I don't mean anyone,' she amended. 'There was just a moment…'

'Okay.'

'Yara was upset. Jasmine reached out for her. I just knew. Women do,' she sneered. 'You wouldn't recognise it if it was in your face.'

'So why are you so upset?'

'Because the two of you used me as some sort of pawn!'

'Absolutely not. Can't you see it would be terrible for Yara for this to get out? For her private life to be publicly dissected?'

'Oh, but it's okay for mine to be?' She was starting to cry and trying hard not to, but felt so embarrassed at how easily she'd succumbed to his charm. 'You used me,' she accused again, 'and I can't bear that I let you. That I didn't see.'

'I was not using you,' Rafiq said, 'Liliana, you *know* what happened that night.'

'I don't know anything anymore. You lied to me. You should have told me.'

'Grow up,' he told her, forgetting he was trying to be nice. 'You know damn well it was not my secret to share. I gave her my word.'

Her breath sucked in. When she thought about it, she did know that. In fact, she was proud of this man whose word was his bond.

'I never lied,' he said. 'So take that back.'

She was a little too proud to do so.

'It was a lie by omission,' Liliana said.

'Really.' Rafiq's smile was incredulous, his face menacingly close, and Mr Nice Guy was out of the window. 'Let's talk about lies by omission, shall we? Is there something *you* haven't told me, Liliana?'

Liliana blinked. She could feel the roar of her pulse in her ears as his eyes bored into her and she wished she could faint or something or run out of the VIP lounge and onto the tarmac. Anything to escape Rafiq's knowing eyes.

'You're pregnant.' Rafiq didn't ask if she was; he told her he knew.

'I—I'm not sure…' she stammered. 'There's a chance,' she admitted.

'Liar,' he said. 'You know damn well. That's the real reason why you ran off at the ball. You weren't scared that I was royal—you just didn't want to tell me.' That smile was pure black. 'And there was me wondering why you were suddenly shy last night when you came to bed. I couldn't work out why you were covering yourself when you'd just bared your…' He stopped himself, and she could feel his ragged breathing on her cheek as perhaps their minds darted to last night. The anger had turned to passion, because the energy between them had changed, and his smile was a different one, slow and sensual, as if he were seducing her right here on this very spot. And doing a rather good job of it actually, because she wanted to kiss that mouth, grab on to him, but the baby was too important for her to lose her thought process to this man.

She needed a calm head and that was impossible when he was near. She had visions of herself in this land, surrounded by children, Rafiq and Yara heading off on royal visits, embroiled in their lies.

'Stay,' he said. 'We'll go back to the desert, we'll get the doctor, take a test…'

He was moving in to kiss her and she didn't know if he was cross or pleased about the baby, or if he even cared.

The hardest thing she had ever done was turn her head and deny Rafiq.

'I have a test with me.'

He released her. 'You haven't taken it?'

'No, I wanted to wait.' She shook her head, unable to look at him.

'Isn't it better that we find out for sure together?' He frowned. 'Liliana, don't deny me this part.'

She nodded and looked around and then slipped away to their private loos.

The loos really were nicer in Rafiq's world.

She did the test and then sat on a high-backed chair,

staring at her pale reflection and wild but still glossy hair, going over what he'd just said.

Don't deny me this part.

He would be there for her.

Rafiq had told her that much.

He would be there in everything and draw her closer and closer to his heart, then shut her out when it suited him. When duty or his suitable wife or non-bastard children called.

She looked down to the indicator and the answer was as expected, the truth she'd tried hard not to know.

Liliana walked out and Rafiq was standing waiting for her but his expression she couldn't read.

'Yes,' she said. 'I am.'

'Wow.' He took the stick from her and stared at the little pink cross, and felt an odd mix of fear and terror, combined with an odd knowing that the gig was up.

That like it or not, love was here.

His thoughts on the subject he would deal with later. Right now, a very pale Liliana came first.

'It's going to be okay.' He drew her into his arms.

And for a moment she leaned on him, breathed him in, and could truly just remain there forever, and let him carry her out and take her back to his desert abode.

Where Rafiq would no doubt tell her how things must be.

No.

She lifted her head, pulled back a touch from his embrace. Her request was the same as it had been moments ago. 'I want to go home.'

'Liliana.' He almost laughed out loud at her request. 'I have just found out you are having my baby.'

'I mean it. You always said I could leave anytime.'

He took a breath, remembering his promise.

Of course she wanted to be at home; perhaps she needed time with her mother, and to just get her head around things. 'Very well.' Reluctantly he released her. 'I'll come and see you in the next few days.'

Rafiq was so arrogant, Liliana thought. So damn sure of himself, so certain that she just needed a few days away to clear her head and then she'd be ready to fall into bed, or to toe the line.

Most terrifying of all, he might just be right. But then she thought of her mother, waiting for a phone call, jumping to her lover's command.

'You don't know me at all, do you?'

'Meaning?'

'I don't want to see you when you're next in London.'

'What do you mean?'

'Just that.' She was shaking inside but she forced her voice steady. 'It would be easier on me if we don't see each other until the baby is born.'

'You're being absurd. You are pregnant with my child. Of course I have to see you—there is a lot to sort out.'

'We can sort things out over the phone, or via email. I shall never keep you from seeing your child.' His eyes narrowed then, and she saw a flash of the warrior she was up against, but Liliana refused to back down. 'I'll never be your mistress, Rafiq.'

'But you know about Yara now. You know why we can't be together just yet…'

'Just yet,' she repeated. 'I think your idea of "just yet" might last for quite some time. Say the next forty years or so…' she continued. 'I think you actually like the edicts,

Rafiq. I think you like playing by the rules—or bending them to suit you.'

'Meaning?'

'Oh, please…' she said and gestured to the lounge, to the scattered cushions on the floor, and he had no idea what she meant but then she continued her speech. 'I think you like the rules, especially when they serve your cold heart well.'

'It's not cold when it's with you.'

'How often will that be?' she challenged, and when he didn't respond, she knew that nothing really had changed. 'Twice a week, or on my birthday, or whenever you can squeeze me unnoticed in?' She refused now to cry. 'Can we walk out of here together?' she asked. 'Can you see me to my plane?'

He didn't answer.

'I thought not.' She was surprisingly calm as she collected her bag. 'Unless you're completely free, I don't want to see you.'

'Careful what you wish for, Liliana,' he warned. 'As you just pointed out, I play by the rules.'

'Meaning?'

'If you say you don't want to see me, you absolutely won't.'

'Good.'

'I shall call for updates about the baby.'

He didn't pull her into his embrace, and neither did he kiss her goodbye.

And although she didn't cry, *this* farewell was the hardest.

CHAPTER THIRTEEN

RAFIQ COULD NEVER be completely free.

While he wasn't officially betrothed, an agreement *had* been reached.

A gentleman's agreement, so to speak. But one made by a prince, a princess and two kings.

At twenty-one it had been easy to give any chance for his heart away, to see Yara's plight and not factor the future in.

At thirty-five he needed a way out of the agreement their fathers had made.

One that didn't compromise Yara.

He could see no way out though.

Rafiq had practically moved into the inner sanctum, poring over the edicts or sometimes just staring at the indicator, the little pink cross that told him he was going to be a father…

The terror he had felt on first finding out had long since gone.

The only fear he had was all he was missing out on, all that Liliana was facing alone.

He stared at the cross, knew she was now sixteen weeks and four days along.

And every day he did not come up with a solution was a day he could never get back.

It was late when the king came in, and he must not have realised Rafiq was in here, for he did an abrupt about-turn. 'I'll go,' the king said. 'I shan't disturb you.'

'It's fine,' Rafiq said.

'No, no, you keep looking for your loophole…'

Rafiq gave a mirthless laugh and got back to searching a scroll.

'I shan't force you,' the king suddenly said. 'And not just because I know that I can't actually force you to marry, but more, you don't deserve it.'

Rafiq nodded. He knew it had taken a lot for his father to say that. 'Thank you.'

They were just unable to speak, both could not meet the other's eyes and Rafiq knew it had to stop. Knew how much better he felt from talking things through with Liliana.

'I understand Khalid now.'

His father halted, but his back remained to his youngest son.

'I thought he had betrayed me. I could not imagine how he could tell them about the tunnel, knowing it would lead to me being taken.'

'We don't know he told them,' the king attempted, but his bark had died and he was tired of avoiding Rafiq's eyes. So, he turned around.

There was no need to hide now for Rafiq had acknowledged the truth out loud.

'I was so ashamed of him,' the king admitted. 'That he let you down, his country…'

'No, please don't think like that of him. I was arrogant,' Rafiq said. 'I thought wild horses wouldn't have dragged information from me. And I thought my scars proved me right.' He closed his eyes, but he thought of his brother and the woman he loved being threatened, and God knows what they had said or done to Khalid.

'But that was then,' Rafiq said. That was before he'd met Liliana, only to change his world. Before he'd resumed feeling. 'I don't know if that's the case now.' He might snap like a twig if it were Liliana under threat, or his child. 'I am sad for what he must have gone through. Don't ever be ashamed of him.'

'I'm not. I was at first, seeing you so injured and weak. I just didn't know how to speak of it with you. With anyone.'

It had rather been erased from records and conversations.

'Rafiq,' his father said, 'I know you think I did nothing to save you…'

'Leave it.'

'No. I did all I could.'

'Of course,' Rafiq said, disbelieving and trying not to show it.

'Do you think the lazy bastard was asleep by accident, or that at the checkpoint the guards simply forgot to check the trunk? I had people watching for you, more than you will ever know. Behind the veil I did all I could.'

Rafiq swallowed as the veil was somewhat lifted.

'The King of Al-Nawar, the current king, did all he could too. He had men on the ground, looking out for you, waiting for you to make a break for freedom, ready to move in and assist…'

'Why did you never say?'

'Many things were lost during those times—open dialogue is often the first thing to go.' He fell quiet.

Rafiq stood, silently accepting that.

'I was about to surrender the troops.' The king admitted a buried truth. 'I was on the edge of that, but then you escaped.'

'You would not have surrendered the troops,' Rafiq refuted. 'I don't believe that.'

'Because you don't allow for love.'

Rafiq exhaled sharply.

'Certainly you don't allow for the love a parent has for their child.'

He was starting to. The thought of a baby, his and Liliana's baby, a world away in London, the thought of them out of reach had him frantically searching for solutions.

'A loving parent will do anything to protect their child,' the king said.

'Not Liliana's father.'

'Then he deserves no thought in this matter.'

Rafiq nodded.

'However, the King of Al-Nawar *is* a loving father.'

Rafiq wasn't sure where his father was going with this. 'Do you mean he understood why you were about to surrender the troops?'

'Rafiq!' The king gave a bark of laughter. 'I never actually told him. If I had, our countries would not now be friends. Thankfully you escaped before it came to that.'

So he attempted open dialogue. 'I know it would have been better had I been the one who died.' Rafiq was not being sentimental or angling for his father to refute. It was simply a fact. 'But I am doing my best. And if I pull out of this arrangement, I'll do all I can not to embarrass Princess Yara or King Al-Nawar.'

'Rafiq,' his father interrupted. 'Why would you think I would have preferred it to be you who died?'

'Because Khalid was born to be king.'

'Yes,' his father agreed. 'But Rafiq, you are a *born* king. A natural leader. You will be like a breath of fresh air.' He looked at him. 'Preferably with a wife and heirs.'

The king knocked on the door to be let out and Khalid stood there frowning. Hadn't he just said he wouldn't force him to marry Yara?

'I shall leave you to your search of the edicts.'

'It's pointless,' Rafiq admitted. 'These are just ancient rules that don't apply to modern times. Believe me…'

'I believe *in* you.' The king interrupted. 'The laws are stubborn, but they are—' then it was the king who was interrupted, the conversation halted, the guards were here and the doors to the sanctum had opened. But before he left, the king turned around '—not quite so ancient.'

Rafiq's tongue was firmly in cheek at the slight rebuke from the king, but then he met his father's eyes and realised he was telling him something.

Some things were too delicate to be stated directly.

Diplomacy ruled, even in the inner sanctum.

'Carry on,' the king said.

'I shall.'

It helped to know that his father was on his side. The moon was too, for it was high in the sky and the pearls were dazzling, making the words leap from the scrolls, and with renewed vigor Rafiq searched for an answer…

To what?

What had his father been pointing to?

There was a subtlety to diplomacy, a way to work within and around the rules.

He thought of Liliana—all he thought of was Liliana these days—but her taunt about him hiding behind the edicts, how the rules suited him irked.

And it still niggled at him.

The way she'd said *oh, please* as she'd gestured to the VIP lounge.

As if speaking about Yara.

And Jasmine.

He replayed his father's words. *Not quite so ancient.*

It really hadn't been a rebuke, instead he was trying to guide him and Rafiq called for the scribe.

'Do we have Al-Nawar's edict amendments?'

'Some,' the scribe said and nodded. 'Only what we can gather, or that are publicly put out.'

'Around the time Khalid was captured.' He thought of when Yara had told him her secret. 'Or a year or so before.'

The scribe thought he was investigating his kidnapping, and Rafiq let him keep it at that.

And there had been a lot of amendments when the king had been overthrown. Small amendments written in fresher ink, but there was nothing that helped him see.

'Let's go back a couple more years,' Rafiq said, his eyes strained, but the moon, swollen and full, had the pearls dazzling, as if directing his finger across the parchment.

And there it was.

A darker ink.

Fresher.

Not so ancient.

'Just minor amendments,' the scribe said as he went through them. 'Mainly regarding the royal retinue and public sightings. Here.' His voice lifted 'A unique lover can be considered for staff.'

'This was Al-Nawar?'

The scribe knew perhaps a little of Rafiq's predicament; he had been in the sanctum for days with him after all. 'I am sure it can be easily done here.'

Rafiq looked up and frowned, realised the scribe thought he was looking for ways to include Liliana in his life.

Rafiq wanted more than that, and Liliana would demand more than that!

'Yes,' Rafiq said, keeping Yara's secret so close that he let the scribe think this was about his own personal predicament.

The veil further lifted.

The King of Al-Nawar did indeed love his daughter, for when she'd been but fifteen, he'd had the foresight to think of her future…

Rafiq was quite sure.

CHAPTER FOURTEEN

LILIANA FELT AS if she were wading through molasses just to get out of bed and walk to the bathroom.

And then wash and dress.

After just a few days off for 'personal reasons' she was back at work.

Taking the tube again had been agony.

There were no photographers waiting for her first day back.

And as good as his word, all the salacious articles had been taken down.

Arriving in the office, all she got was a nice smile from Margo, who she'd expected to fall on her neck and demand the gossip, only no-one had questions.

She rather guessed that Rafiq had taken care of that too.

Simon came over. 'Good to see you back, Liliana.' He nodded and walked off.

It was as if Rafiq had never arrived at the ball. As if there had been no scandal, no photos. It was as if their time together had been erased.

Normal life slowly returned, except it could never go back, because she was pregnant with his baby and in love with the unattainable.

At night, she would love to say she'd started sewing, with some of the gorgeous fabrics he'd gifted her.

Proving to him and herself that she intended to go it alone.

Only she didn't want to be alone.

Taking the tube home at the end of her workday was the worst.

A few times she just sat there, let the tube rattle on and take her through tunnels and flashes of blue sky above ground, but it seemed paler than the skies in the desert.

Then the announcement would come—they were at the end of the line.

Occasionally he called.

'Liliana?'

Her heart leapt at the sound of his voice.

'Rafiq.'

It felt luxurious to say his name,

There were no endless messages, or flowers or anything, just short calls and polite requests—that she see a private doctor, which she just had for the second time.

'How was the doctor's visit?'

'It went well.' She nodded. 'Everything looks fine.'

'What does that mean?'

'My blood results and such, and he did an ultrasound. There'll be another at twenty-one weeks. That's in five weeks' time.'

'I can count Liliana, and I have not forgotten how far along you are.'

'Of course.'

He was very polite and businesslike, and she secretly hoped he would suggest being there for the next ultrasound, but he didn't.

'Is it moving?'

'No,' she said. 'Well, I could see it moving on the screen, and kicking and such, but it's too soon for me to feel it yet.'

He was silent.

In fact, Rafiq pressed the bridge of his nose between his thumb and forefinger and fought for control.

'How's your manager?' he asked in a voice that sounded a bit cross, but he was trying to hold things in.

'He's being very polite.'

'Excellent.'

'What did you say to him?' she asked. 'To everyone? Nobody's even mentioned the ball.'

He didn't respond.

Rafiq, Liliana had long since decided, was very comfortable with silence.

'Things seem calmer with you too.' She filled in the gap, terrified he'd end the call. 'I meant between the countries. I read that progress is being made with the cultural exchange—you're meeting with the King of Al-Nawar.'

'I don't discuss such matters on an open line.'

'Of course not.'

'And, given you would rather not see me until the baby is here, I cannot go into detail.'

'Rafiq, when I said that…' She swallowed, telling herself that she meant it, trying so hard not to give in. She had calmed down, of course. If anything she was proud of him for keeping Yara's secret. Oh, she was so tempted to back down. To tell him she'd been wrong.

But then she thought of her mother, sitting by the phone, waiting for the master to call.

It was Rafiq who broke the long silence. 'You meant it.'

'Yes, but I lie a lot, remember.'

Rafiq gave her nothing. 'I ought to go. Call me if you need anything.'

'Do you want…?' She paused. 'I have some photos from today's ultrasound. Should I send them?'

'Sure.'

'I don't know if you…' she started but he had already rung off and she had no idea when she would hear from him again.

Oh, he should have been here today, at the doctor's with her. She could have had that; he could have been here in London for this day, and right now every day that was without him felt a day that was too long.

Perhaps she had been too presumptuous, Liliana thought as the tears came. Perhaps when a future king offers you *almost* everything, you should be very certain you mean it when you scorn his offers.

Because she did want to see him again, desperately; instead he respected her wishes.

Just a little too completely.

Rafiq would respect her wishes completely.

He knew she was weakening, God knows he was too, but he was determined not to see her until he had put things right.

His phone bleeped a message and two black-and-white images came onto his screen. One was a still image; he looked at the profile and the curve of spine, and the little hands and feet. And the next, he pressed and watched their baby moving, little hands waving and a tiny mouth opening and closing, and then it seemed to push off, like a swimmer kicking from the pool wall.

And everything in his life seemed to hang on to today.

'Your Highness. Your flight is ready.'

'Thank you.'

He turned off the image on his phone.

And headed to Al-Nawar.

Oh, she missed him so much. She thought of what he'd once said: I am not your father. And he wasn't. Rafiq was a deep and complex man and they had, she was sure, fallen in love.

The tears fell harder then, and she let them, and they came with big gulps of self-recrimination, for she should have been careful what she wished for, because she had fallen in love with a man who respected her wishes.

Who kept his word.

Liliana truly fought not to call him back, to retract. She was sobbing into tissues. As her mother had.

Then later she sat watching the news and all the pomp of Crown Prince Rafiq arriving in Al-Nawar to a cheering crowd, being welcomed by the stony-faced king. She kept bracing herself for the announcement, to officially hear that Rafiq and Yara were betrothed.

Instead, she watched as he rode alongside a miserable king in a motorcade to the palace, past the cheering crowds with Rafiq by his side.

They were inside for a couple of hours, and then appeared on the steps of the palace to shake hands.

And Rafiq had surely caved to the two kings' commands, because the king was now smiling.

So she sobbed her way through a complicated translation and found out that yes, agreements had been made, though for what she didn't quite know.

And then she stopped.

Liliana stopped because she didn't want history to repeat. And just as Rafiq had said he was not her father, she didn't have to be like her mother either. She blew her nose and sat up on the edge of the bed, already regretting the headache her crying jag would cause.

And she refused to be reliant on Rafiq for her happiness, for her money, and right now she was being a pathetic drip, but she was proud of herself too.

For saying no to him.

For refusing to fold.

For not settling for less.

She stood and examined herself in the mirror. The pale blue shift dress she had bought to disguise her bump no longer hung well. It was a little tight across the bust and hips and when she turned to the side she could see the soft swell of her belly.

There had been a few glances at work, but whatever Rafiq or his office or whoever had said, meant that noone had asked. Not even Margo, who she'd used to gossip with.

Before Rafiq.

Everything felt like a before and after.

Before she'd been happy and lively; now she stood, all bloated and red, and pathetic. And she hadn't been like that—she'd cared about pretty dresses and shoes, and the old Liliana would not have lain idle with ream upon ream of gorgeous fabrics sitting in her spare room.

It was out with the tape measure and off with her bra, and she yelped when she saw just how much she'd grown.

Not just her bust, and not just her hips, but in herself. She could manage without him. Somehow their time had made her stronger.

If she could stand up to an arrogant crown prince she could deal with anything…

And look fabulous while doing so!

She looked through the fabrics, her hand reaching for one, but then again pink really could be problematic, and it just might make her cry. Then a gorgeous silk caught her eye, a deep orange, and she reached for some sheer chiffon in the palest peach, the very palest peach, and layered the two in her hands.

They were perfect.

She made a simple shift slip from the silk, and then spent hours perfecting the chiffon and when she awoke the next morning it was hanging from her wardrobe. Like a pale desert sunrise, Liliana thought, not that she'd actually seen one.

Maybe a desert sunset.

Except she'd been too busy being made love to by Rafiq to see one.

Instead of crying, she let the memory make her smile.

Liliana had a wonderful job, well, not really, but there *were* wonderful perks, like wearing stunning clothes for work.

'Wow!' Margo said. 'You look…' She smiled.

'Better?' Liliana offered.

'Better,' Margo agreed. 'Like a mango ice cream.'

'Thank you!'

Margo had sat beside her in recent weeks, and offered

not words of advice, because she had no idea what was going on, but quiet support.

'Did you make that one too?'

'I did.'

'Can you make one for me?'

She had never asked by one of her colleagues before.

'Seriously,' Margo said picking up the chiffon and admiring it. 'Though hopefully I'll get a discount, given we're friends.'

Margo wasn't merely asking her to make one, but offering to pay her for it.

And given where they worked and their passions for high fashion it was rather a big deal.

'I'll give you a discount.' Liliana smiled, so pleased to have friends.

'Dress by Liliana.' Margo winked.

With a little help from Rafiq.

He really had given her the most wonderful gift, and it tore at her heart that he could be so thoughtful at times and yet so remote at others.

It was a busy day, answering emails and taking calls, and she was just starting to flag from all this positivity, just trying to remember her vow to return to the Liliana of before. With additions. A baby on the way, and a heart she was determined to mend.

It was close to four, and she was just about to sag, just about to reach for her phone in the hope she'd missed his call, when Margo appeared over her computer screen.

'Your sexy prince is about to give a live interview.'

'He's not *my* sexy prince,' Liliana said, but of course she looked up to the endless screens, and found him in a split second.

Oh, he looked utterly beautiful, wearing a dark charcoal-grey suit and a gunmetal tie, and her longing for more details had her stand and walk over and just blatantly stare.

A longing for more detail must have overtaken the entire office. It would seem no embargo from Rafiq was going to stop her colleagues from hearing this.

'I can't help myself,' Margo said, working the main remote, and in a matter of seconds, Rafiq filled every screen and the mute button was pressed and there was his deep calm voice.

Talking flowers.

Or rather, rare veiled orchids, found mainly on Yara's island.

'The King of Al-Nawar just wanted assurances,' Rafiq said, and started talking about some cultural exchange. It would be boring if it wasn't Rafiq. He made everything, *everything* fascinating! 'We will of course protect the ecosystem—there was never any question as to that.'

It sounded as if they were back in agreement—more that they were working together to improve both lands' tourism industry.

Blah, blah, blah…

She wasn't listening for that, more for the sound of his voice and the dark of his eyes. He looked exquisite. Very austere and sometimes his eyes flashed a warning at the interviewer when they tried to move the topic onto more personal ones.

And she truly didn't know where he was.

The interviewer was American, so he might be there, and at the table by his chair there were said veiled orchids, and she wondered if he was at the palace, or even in Al-Nawar.

'You were recently photographed in London,' the interviewer said.

And then he flashed *that* look—the one that could halt a meteor and cause it even to revert, but then he swallowed and gave a short nod of permission for the interviewer to continue.

'Your actions surely caused great embarrassment to all parties?'

'Unintentionally,' Rafiq agreed. 'But that has all been resolved.'

'Did you apologise to Princess Yara?'

'Princess Yara said I owe her no apology.'

'What about the King of Al-Nawar, did you apologise to him for your actions?'

Rafiq shot another look, one that should have shattered that meteorite into millions of little pieces. It was such a look that even Simon stepped back. Perhaps he'd been the recipient of it once before. And Liliana found herself give a little giggle at the very thought, but then it faded as Rafiq cleared his throat.

'I did not,' he told the interviewer.

'So how can things be better if you have not apologised?'

'I refuse to apologise for falling in love.'

Liliana froze, unsure quite what those words meant.

Then she looked at his eyes and he was looking directly at the camera, defiant. Determined.

She didn't know what it meant—for if those words were somehow for her…was it a one-off declaration?

Whatever it was, her heart was leaping from her chest to her throat.

'Liliana,' Margo said and nudged her. 'You have a visitor.'

Turning her head towards the main glass doors and seeing him, Liliana frowned and then looked back to the screen, where the interviewer was wrapping things up. So the interview mustn't have been completely live, because there Rafiq was. Wearing the same charcoal suit from the television and the same immaculate tie.

But honestly, seeing him in the flesh, the mango ice cream was in danger of melting…

Her first thought was unintelligible. Even Liliana's own brain couldn't decipher it: a mixture of joy and relief to see him, and hope, and simply that he was here. Rafiq, the person her heart recognised.

Her second thought was terribly vain—thank goodness he hadn't appeared yesterday!

Every day was precious, every day could be a lesson and while, yes, she could survive without him, life was so much better when he was close.

She wanted to run to him—no, she wanted to fly into his arms, but he was not one for public displays, and more so now, neither was she.

'Two minutes,' she mouthed and then put two fingers up, and then fervently hoped she hadn't just given him a rude sign, but clearly not, because he gave a simple nod.

'Er, Simon.' It was her now slinking over to him. 'Would it be possible to finish a little early today? I do have a few hours in the bank.'

'No problem,' Simon said, his face bright red, and then

she glanced over to Margo, who was smiling brightly and gave her a wink.

And somehow, she went and turned off her computer, calmly. As if every head in the office wasn't turning between her and Rafiq as if they were watching a tennis match. Somehow she was outwardly calm as she collected her bag, as if there wasn't a crown prince standing at the door, waiting for her to join him. Somehow, she walked to Rafiq when she wanted to run.

'Hi.' She smiled. 'I *really* wasn't expecting to see you today.'

'That almost troubles me,' Rafiq responded with a smile of his own.

She looked incredible, almost better without him than with, but then he saw the slightly puffy eyes and the slight tremble on her lips, and he knew…

He just knew.

This was love.

He was utterly relieved to see her, and proud to see her gorgeous and smiling when he was certain she had been hurting just as badly as he had. Now, seeing her safe and radiant, he could finally allow himself to be excited too about the baby beneath her floaty, stunning dress.

'I was hoping you could get away a little early,' he said.

'All sorted.'

'Excellent.' He nodded and extended his arm in a this-way gesture rather than taking hers. 'My driver is waiting, though at the private exit.'

He wouldn't be so tacky as to arrive at the front entrance.

She took the busy elevator down, and they stood together, not touching, not smiling into each other's eyes, not anything, but together.

Liliana could not wait to be alone with him. Her lips ached for his kiss, her body was alive and she would be a liar if she said she wasn't going to sleep with him.

The sight of him was divine, the scent of him sublime, and just his strong presence made the world feel right as they walked out to the waiting car,

They drove through busy London streets, and there was no passionate kiss in the back of the car, not even a brush of fingers.

'Your interview went well,' she said, hoping for a little more of a clue.

'Thank you.' He nodded. 'We shall discuss it later.'

He turned to look out of the window, and she realised that even in a blacked-out limousine with his own driver, still Rafiq did not let down his guard. Liliana was starting to realise what a complete exception their first date had been. She only saw the real Rafiq when they were alone.

Surely they would be soon? But no, they were leaving central London. At first she had assumed they would be going to his home, or even her own, but no, as the car turned at an exit, as the roads became winding, the view becoming ever greener, she knew where he was taking her: to the stately home where he had made her his.

And she was through lying to herself. Liliana knew she was his mistress already, because even if he did have to marry Yara…

Her breath caught.

Rafiq had been right to tell her to grow up. Well, he

could have said it more nicely, she thought, sneaking a look at him, but she was proud he'd kept that difficult secret.

Oh, she was worried about Yara. If her refusal to go along with things meant the princess was in trouble…

There were two men dressed in dark suits as they entered the driveway towards the carriage house. 'There's a lot of security,' she murmured. 'They must have someone…' And then her lips snapped closed and she realised the suited men were there for them.

She looked at the lake where they had first kissed. The swans were squabbling, standing on the water and flapping their wings, angrily turning, then gliding away from the other and elegant again…

Oh, Rafiq.

She had thought he had forgotten her. That distance had somehow severed their bond, yet he was like one of those swans, working beneath the surface, outwardly unruffled.

They stepped out, and the concierge greeted them politely and then they were discreetly escorted for the longest walk, up staircases, and then Rafiq thanked the gentleman and she could feel his impatience as he took the key.

'Thank God,' he breathed when they were finally alone.

'Oh, Rafiq.' She needed details, to know all that was going on, but she had left them to him. They could stay there for just a little while more, because she was back in his arms and they were kissing. Back where she had longed to be and increasingly naked with the man to whom her heart belonged.

He undressed her, taking in the changes, kissing her shoulder, exploring her breasts, caressing her bump.

'I was nervous when I found out.'

'Really?'

'Terrified,' he admitted. 'I knew the gig was up.' He kissed her. 'I was going to be in love, like it or not.' He ran the back of his hand over the swell of her stomach. 'I like it.'

'And me.'

He shrugged off his jacket as she loosened his tie, and they were kissing and her hands were on his wide shoulders.

His mouth would forever be too exciting to be familiar, and she undid the buttons of his shirt, and then swallowed, her hands meeting the wall of muscle.

'Oh, my God…'

Her body wasn't the only one with changes.

She stripped him with the glee of a Christmas present, undid his belt as if it were annoying tape.

Magnificent before, he was stunning now, sort of rippling with health and muscle and she ran a hand on his very flat stomach and down to solid thighs.

'You've been running.'

'Yeah.'

'A lot.'

'A lot…' he admitted. 'When I can't stand that you are not here, I go to the desert and I run.'

He was all masculine energy and she felt a little wobbly, but he adored her with his hands…

'I missed you…' She kept saying it between kisses, and kept saying it as he reclaimed her.

They made love side on, their legs scissored, and able to touch each other, to kiss, to rediscover each other.

'Never do that again,' he said, taking her deep. 'Seriously, Liliana.'

It had been weeks.

She was breathless, but he was not. He took everything she had to give.

Made her say his name before he came.

'Say it…' he told her.

'Rafiq,' she begged, and she told him something else as she came. 'I love you.'

They lay silent, coming down; even Rafiq was a bit breathless.

And should she have said she loved him?

Too needy? she thought, because he hadn't said it back.

'Too much?' she asked and he turned and smiled.

'I love hearing it.'

He pulled her in, and as he'd wanted to that first day, dropped a kiss on her head.

'I missed you,' she said.

'I know you did,' Rafiq said. 'But I'm here now.'

He didn't say it back, and then laughed when she dug him in the ribs.

And who knows where they led…

Right now, she was here.

'Is Yara okay?'

'Seriously?' Rafiq teased, 'I turn up at your work, I bring you here, we make love and that is your question?'

'I'm worried for her and Jasmine.' She took a breath. 'I understand that you might have to marry. I don't like it, but…' She had sworn to never compromise, to never back down. Only this didn't feel like that; it felt too right for that.

'Stop,' Rafiq said. 'You told me to sort it, and I have. I have been in long talks with the King of Al-Nawar. He knows my stance about apologising, and now so does the world—I told him when we met that I shan't apologise for falling in love. Do you know what he said?'

'No.'

'Nor should anyone have to.'

'Do you think he knows?'

'I am almost certain.' He smiled. 'You put me in the right direction. Yara and Jasmine are seen together. To have your lover as part of your retinue is forbidden in Al-Zahir, but in Al-Nawar the laws were amended a few years ago. There are no restrictions on being seen with your lover there.'

'Yara's father changed them?'

'I believe so, and I believe not without an awful lot of thought and love. I don't quite know how it happened, but I know my father was trying to lead me to it.'

'Why would he be pushing for you to marry her?'

'I think he guessed I knew. He trusts me to take care of her.' He lay there, arranging himself on his thigh. 'I can't tell you all that was said in the inner sanctum, but he knows I shall always do my best by Yara. But you and the baby come first.'

Liliana lay there, loving the feel of his hand on her stomach as he stroked the soft skin, as he acknowledged the little life inside.

'The baby has grown.'

'I have too,' Liliana said. 'I know we can't be married…'

'Why not?'

'It would cause offence.'

'Not now.'

'Your country would never accept me.'

'My country is thrilled to see me happy.' He pulled her into him. 'They want the countries to move forward in unison. Did you notice the flowers by my side at the interview?' He rolled his eyes. 'I have been speaking orchids and fauna and eco…' He groaned.

'That was when I knew I loved you,' Liliana admitted. 'I knew that I could talk about flowers with you.'

'Liliana, it nearly killed me when you couldn't tell me about the baby. I never want you to feel that way again,'

'No.' She shook her head. 'I wasn't scared of your reaction or anything like that. I was worried about…' She gestured to the bed. 'This. I knew if I stayed, I might never leave.'

'Get dressed.'

'I want to stay here.'

'Get dressed,' he told her.

He had something he needed to say.

Properly.

They walked together through the grounds, not so much as holding hands, around the side of the gorgeous mansion and down a cobbled lane until they came to a gate. There was no padlock on the walled rose garden. The scent was incredible, and there were beds of lemons and apricot and bold reds, buds ready to pop open and some in full flower, and there was a little robin sitting on a high wall and singing as he led her down the next row.

He really did things properly; he was down on one knee and holding a polished wooden box.

'Liliana, will you marry me?'

'Marriage?'

He nodded.

'Just us? I mean…'

'Just us. Forever.'

It was a pearl, so perfect, and set high with two diamonds on each side, as if guarding its beauty,

'It is a pearl farmed on the day I was born.' Rafiq explained its meaning. 'It is yours forever now. If you accept it, you must take it to your grave.' He grimaced. 'Sorry, I have to say that.'

She laughed, her eyes too full with happy tears. And she was straight back into his embrace and kiss, and of course the answer was yes.

She didn't even need to say it.

Surely?

Oh, but she did.

'Yes?' Rafiq checked.

'Of course.'

'You will marry me?'

'Yes!'

'So we are betrothed.' He held her close and in the fragrant rose garden she found a little more of their impossible but beautiful ways. 'Then I can say it now. I love you, Liliana. My heart turned to you on the night we met.'

The terminology didn't sound strange to her now, for it was exactly how she felt. 'And my heart turned to you.'

EPILOGUE

HIS LIFE REALLY was a succession of anniversaries.

And even if it was nine months to the day since he'd escaped, there were other dates on the calendar of his life now.

In a few moments she would be a whole day old.

Princess Sahar of Al-Zahir lay in her little Perspex crib.

Not a care in the world.

As it should be.

And for as long as he could, that would remain.

The king and queen had been in yesterday, to meet their brand-new granddaughter, and they were trying to sort out the edicts so she would one day be queen.

Rafiq did not even want to think about that!

Liliana's mother was enjoying her stay at the palace.

Very much!

The King of Al-Nawar was too weak to visit. But Princess Yara, to show both countries there was no hard feelings, would be visiting later today.

But right now, it was the lovely quiet of dawn.

She had soft black hair and blue eyes, ten fingers and ten toes and they were both enchanted.

Sahar.

It meant *new dawn* or *sunrise*, as it had been when she'd been born…

It was sunrise now. This very modern prince had, the news had reported, stayed at the hospital overnight.

The people were thrilled to see their crown prince happy again and restored to his charming self.

'What are you doing?' Liliana asked sleepily as he wandered around the royal suite, reading cards, picking up pink teddies, sort of pacing.

'Waiting for her to wake up,' he said. 'Go back to sleep.'

Instead, she looked over to the crib and saw Sahar stirring a little, her hand peeking out from the wrap.

She knew what this day was.

They had even half joked that she might come on the anniversary of his escape, but she was quietly pleased she hadn't. This day, for Rafiq, was, despite what everyone thought, a difficult one.

How it could have ended still flashed through his mind.

'I can't believe she's here,' Liliana sighed, waking up to the sight of her baby, and her little snub nose and rosebud mouth.

It had been a gorgeous birth.

Quiet and calm and the midwife used to be a hurdle champion, of all things.

Only Rafiq didn't answer, and she realised he'd stopped pacing.

She rolled over and he stood, very still, holding a little doll, reading a card, yet she could not read the expression on his face.

'What is it?' Liliana asked and he turned and looked at her.

'"*Lur da kur jannat da…*"' Rafiq, said then translated. '"A daughter is the paradise of the home. With blessings from my happy family to yours." It's unsigned.' He looked over and explained what the card meant. 'It's from Balach…'

That card meant so much, she knew.

Liliana sat up in bed as he came over, and putting the little dolly in the crib he picked up Sahar and gazed at her for a very long time.

'I can't believe she's here either,' Rafiq said, then looked up at her. 'Or you.'

'Well, I am.' Liliana smiled, though she knew what he meant. She had to pinch herself at times to believe he was near.

He climbed on the bed, balancing their baby with ease, and stretched out beside her.

Their baby between them watching a desert sunrise.

The sky painted pink as if for them.

'Pink can be problem—' she started.

'No,' Rafiq said. 'Pink is perfect.'

He would not have it any other way.

* * * * *

Were you captivated by His Forbidden Royal Heir?
Then you're certain to love these other intensely emotional stories by Carol Marinelli.

Virgin's Stolen Nights with the Boss
Bride Under Contract
She Will Be Queen
Italian's Pregnant Mistress
Italian's Cinderella Temptation

Available now!